JoAnn Aitken has lived all her life in Hamilton, Ontario. She worked for many years at a local community college and has always enjoyed travel. A 2015 trip to Ireland brought together some ideas which became *Family Portraits*. She describes writing the book as "easy" once she got started. As the end of the story approached, she found it hard to let go. She hopes her readers will feel the same.

JoAnn Aitken

Family Portraits

Austin Macauley Publishers™
London • Cambridge • New York • Sharjah

Ordering Information:
Quantity sales: special discounts are available on quantity purchases by corporations, associations, and others. For details, contact the publisher at the address below.

Publisher's Cataloging-in-Publication data
Aitken, JoAnn
Family Portraits

ISBN 9781643780092 (Paperback)
ISBN 9781643780108 (Hardback)
ISBN 9781645366713 (ePub e-book)

The main category of the book — Fiction / Romance / Contemporary

Library of Congress Control Number: 2019908442

www.austinmacauley.com/us

First Published (2019)
Austin Macauley Publishers LLC
40 Wall Street, 28th Floor
New York, NY 10005
USA

mail-usa@austinmacauley.com
+1 (646) 5125767

"Jesus, Finn…you fucking my sister on the supper table?" Ronnie leaned in the archway, eating a cookie.

Finn straightened up with a start and quickly pulled himself together. He had been far away, lost in his young wife, transported by her warm breath on his neck and her whispered words of love in his ear.

"What are you doing here? We didn't expect you until late."

"I live here, Finn, if you will recall." Ronnie popped the last bite of cookie into his month and headed for the stairs. "Just came home to change. I won't be long." He looked at his little sister who was covered up now and sat with her face hidden against her new husband's chest.

He felt sorry for his intrusion, albeit unintentional, and said as he started upstairs, "I know you're married but three weeks. I'll not say a word."

The Gallaghers

January 1970

Finnegan Gallagher was twenty-five years old, tall and extremely handsome, not that he noticed or cared. He was bright, well-educated, and well-traveled. He had studied for a year at Trinity College with the intention of becoming an engineer, but yearning to see more of the world, he left school and went to the continent of Europe.

That was his real education. He was a great reader of history and geography books. He enjoyed studying atlases. Actually being in the places he had read about brought him deep satisfaction.

Everywhere he went, he observed construction of some sort going on. Everywhere he saw cranes at work, and he decided to go to London to train as a crane operator. He figured that would allow him to travel pretty much anywhere, including Canada where he thought he might like to settle. He had an older brother, an engineer at a large Ontario steel mill, who had urged him many times to emigrate.

Crane operating was perfect for Finn. He was calm and meticulous, responsible and moderate in his ways. He could take direction while, at the same time, possessing strong leadership skills. Simply put, he was a dream employee.

In 1969, he returned to his childhood home of Killarney to stay with his mother who was terminally ill. He found a job, but after his mother passed away, he wanted to leave Killarney behind permanently. In November, he moved to Cobh, closer to the sea, closer to his goal of going to Canada.

He immediately got an operator's job at a ship building company and a room in a local boarding house. He liked the job, and his supervisor liked him.

Unfortunately, Finn's boarding house was filled with rowdy young men who liked to drink and fight. Finn himself lived quietly and frugally. He went to bed early. The nature of his job required that he be in the best shape every day; people's lives depended on him.

He kept to himself and didn't go to the pubs. He spent a lot of time at the library and walked the countryside around Cobh. He looked to the west and tried to imagine himself in Canada. He hoped to fly out the following year.

He was increasingly annoyed with the noise and ruckus at the house. One day in mid-January, the boys were drunk and out of control and threw a couch through the front window. Finn had had enough and talked to his supervisor, "Mac" McGuiness, asking for a suggestion as to where he might go.

Mac sat quiet for a minute or two and then said, "Our Patrick got married not long ago, and his room is empty. Would you consider boarding with us? Of course I would have to talk to my wife, but I've already mentioned you, and I believe she will welcome you." Finn was grateful and said so.

The next day, Mac suggested that Finn drop by the house to meet his wife, Mary Frances, and see the room. Finn was optimistic and knocked on the McGuiness front door after work that very afternoon.

A lovely young girl crowned with braids of shining strawberry blonde hair answered and said, "You must be Finn. I am Molly." She shook his hand and called to her mother.

Mary Frances was nice, the room was nice, and the deal was struck. Finn had found a new home.

It was a happy home such as Finn had never known personally.

Mac and Mary Frances were firm but loving with their children. They had three sons: Patrick, recently married to Eileen; Daniel, who worked at the shipyard; Ronald, the joshing cut-up, who drove truck for a company which made shipping containers. And then there was their adored baby, Mary Margaret, Molly. Molly was her mother's assistant and helped with all the household chores in addition to attending secondary school.

She was a capable girl, endlessly patient with her brothers' incessant, good-natured teasing. But, when pushed too far, she could give as good as she got. Ronnie was particularly unrelenting, and legend had it that she had once chased him out of the house with a rolling pin in hand. She was so mature that Finn took her for about seventeen. She was, in fact, only fifteen.

He was enchanted by her natural beauty and sweetness, and she was in silent awe of everything about him. Mac and Mary Frances watched in amusement the secret glances they stole at each other, always quickly averting their eyes when the other looked in their direction.

"Can you feel the chemistry at the dinner table, my dear," Mac asked Mary Frances. "'Tis a powerful thing indeed," she replied. "But Molly is ten years younger than Finn, and he will be gone to Canada in little more than a year's time."

"Love always finds a way," Mac replied, "As you well know." He patted her hand, and she laughed and gave him a kiss.

"We shall see what we shall see," Mary Frances said.

By March, Finn could think of little but Molly. Only when he was working could he focus on anything else. In the night when he couldn't sleep, he would mentally compose poems about her.

A recurring image in those compositions was her beautiful big brown eyes. Sometimes he compared her to a playful puppy, other times a delicate fawn. He feared he was going crazy and more than once packed his bags in the middle of the night only to unpack them in the morning before he left for work.

He finally recognized that he couldn't carry on this way, and he talked to Mac. "I love your daughter, Mac," he said, "and I'm asking your permission to court her with the intention of marriage."

Mac managed to keep a straight face. "I know no better man than you, Finn. But you'll be remembering that Molly is only fifteen. And you are planning on going to Canada."

"I know she's young, but she's mature beyond her years. As far as Canada goes, I would be willing to put it on the back burner until she felt ready or abandon the idea altogether if she didn't want to go. And if she doesn't want me, I will leave your home and bother her no more."

"Well, boy, I know that I speak for Mary Frances too when I tell you to make your move. But please take it slow and gentle with her. She's never had anything to do with the opposite sex, so she may be timid."

"I promise I will treat her like a tiny fawn," Finn said, using his own imagery.

When they had gone to bed, Mac told Mary Frances about Finn's request, and she was delighted. "She thinks he is a miracle of wonderfulness."

Finn's "tiny fawn" promise made her misty-eyed, and Mac thought to himself, *That boy's not going to have any problem. We've got a wedding to look forward to.*

After the dishes were washed, Finn went into the kitchen. "I'm going to the library to return some books. Would you care to walk with me, Molly?"

She blushed. "I want to, Finn, but I'm working on an assignment I just can't get. It's about physics."

"I know something about physics," he said modestly. "Maybe I could give you some pointers, if you would like."

"Oh, please," she replied eagerly.

"Well, get your textbook and the assignment, and come along." And so she did.

Finn had the ability to explain difficult subjects clearly and succinctly. He was impressed by how her nimble mind grasped the concepts. He was thrilled by her closeness as she bent over her notebook. He was intoxicated by the smell of her hair.

The evening was a great success. She was enthralled. He was besotted. It was the first of many evenings, some spent at the library, some just walking together as the spring flowers came into bloom.

She was unlike any girl he had ever known. She wasn't vain or coy. She wasn't needy or demanding. She had no agenda. She talked simply of her love for her family and the community where she had lived all her life. But she also expressed a curiosity about the rest of the world, a subject which forged another link in their unspoken connection.

One night he invited her to see a movie. In the darkened theatre, he took her hand, and he held it until they got home. "You are very special to me, Molly," he said softly and kissed her very gently.

"I never dreamed I would know someone like you," she replied.

"Let's talk some more tomorrow," he suggested and she smiled and nodded.

In the wink of an eye, it was mid-May. The wholesome little romance continued. Finn was exercising a great deal of restraint as he wooed her like a tiny fawn. It wasn't easy, and he planned to propose to her as soon as he could summon the courage.

After a sunset concert at the pavilion, they walked home by the harbor. Finn asked her to sit for a while with him, and then he declared himself. He took her hand and said, "Molly, my beautiful one, I have loved you from the time I moved into your family's house. I can't hold back any longer, and I am asking if you would consider being my wife."

Her eyes widened with surprise, and then she said, "I love you more than anything, and I want to be with you forever." In his elation, Finn gave her her first real kiss and held her in his arms. "Now we have to tell your parents."

"My parents adore you," she said. "Let's go and tell them right away."

Mac and Mary Frances were watching television in the parlor. Molly said, "Mommy and Daddy, Finn has asked me to marry him, and I said yes. This is the happiest night of my life, and I hope you're happy too." They were.

Finn said, "We agreed that Molly should finish the school year. That will be on June 15. With your permission, we would like to be wed the following Friday, June 22."

Mary Frances burbled with excitement, and Mac shook Finn's hand and said, "Good on you, boy." Finn uncharacteristically beamed with delight.

June 21, 1970

After meeting with the priest to talk about the next day's details, Finn and Molly walked hand in hand on the pathway by Cork Harbor through the deepening dusk. Finn noticed that Molly was lagging behind a little and shortened his long strides. He looked at her and asked, "What is it, my dear?"

"I don't want to wait until tomorrow, Finn. I want to be yours now. There's no one around." It was a bold declaration for such a virginal young girl.

"But we must wait until tomorrow. I'll not take you in a hedgerow like a common trollop. It's just not right nor worthy of you," he said and gently pulled her forward in the direction of home.

It was silent as they walked until she asked, "Do you think I'm awful?"

He turned and faced her. "Awful? You can't imagine how much I love you and want you." With that, he pulled her into his arms. It was no sweet kiss this time. He kissed her hungrily, like a starving man, and she responded. He clasped her breast, and she gasped and shuddered against him.

He forced himself to stop and backed away. She looked shaken, her lips swollen, all color drained from her face. "We'll finish this tomorrow," he said in what he hoped was a steady voice. "Now come along. I've got to get you home before I do something I'll regret."

He led her home rapidly, mentally cursing himself for losing control. She kept up, dazzled by what had happened. She had never imagined such a feeling.

On the porch, he kissed her gently. "Good night, my darling. This time tomorrow, our bodies and souls will be joined forever."

Then he hurried away. He was expected at the Fox and Fiddle for a couple of pints with Mac and the boys, but first he stopped briefly in the Silver Swan to compose himself. He was to spend the night at Patrick's, a merciful blessing after all his sleepless nights pacing the floor, knowing that everything he wanted in the world was just across the hall.

June 22, 1970

The members of Molly's immediate family gathered at the Cathedral in the late afternoon to witness her marriage to Finn. Although she was only fifteen years old, no one had any reservations. They all considered Finn to be a man without equal. As Ronnie put it, "Our Moll's hit the jackpot."

Mac presented his radiant daughter to Finn, and in a few minutes it was done. Finn, a man known for his calm and dignified demeanor, was blatantly joyous and gazed at his bride with adoration. Molly clung to his arm and looked up at him worshipfully. They were all alone in the world.

It was a beautiful day, and the family and some friends attended a small reception in Patrick and Eileen's garden. Finn and Molly never left each other's side until it was time for them to go.

The family members had made arrangements to spend that night and the next elsewhere. The house was theirs, and Finn scooped Molly up in his arms and carried her over the threshold. She giggled in delight, and he took her face in his hands. The passion of the previous night was now a raging conflagration.

He led her upstairs to his room, and their magical journey had begun.

The honeymoon went on and on, even after the family returned home. Molly's innocence thrilled Finn beyond anything he had ever experienced.

She had no hang-ups or attitudes; she made no judgments. She was open to anything he suggested or showed her. She was wildly responsive to him. He was a lost man.

Finn was amazed that his love for her grew stronger every day. Molly was certain that, somehow, he was God. Not surprisingly, before long she was pregnant.

Molly made the announcement at a family dinner in honor of her sixteenth birthday after her mother brought out the special cake she had made for the occasion.

After the applause and congratulatory toasts, she sat on a sublimely happy Finn's lap as he fed her forkfuls of birthday cake. This was the same man who, not so long ago, had been viewed by many as taciturn and aloof. A fifteen-year-old girl had changed everything.

March 31, 1971

Mac and his sons waited at the pub with Finn as Molly delivered their child. Her labor had begun in the afternoon, and Finn was a wreck, to the great amusement of the other men. They had never seen him like this.

The last half of her pregnancy had been an emotional rollercoaster for him. Although his wife was young and strong, not gaining much weight and placidly carrying on with her regular routine right up to the end, he was filled with terror.

When they lay in bed and he kissed and caressed her belly and she stroked his hair, he felt calm and in control of himself. Other times, he would wake up drenched with sweat from nightmares about something gone awry. He knew without question that he couldn't live without her and flogged himself for being the cause of her potential demise.

Not allowed to be with her when she drew her last breath, he spent this evening sitting in a darkened corner of the pub with his head in his hands. He prayed to a God he didn't believe existed. He wouldn't drink any alcohol, although Mac urged him to at least take a shot of whiskey to steady his nerves.

After what seemed like an eternity, Paddy, the bar man, clanged the bell: "Finnigan Gallagher, you have a son. Your wife is fine and is asking for you." The patrons cheered, and Finn bolted for the door.

Patrick (to honor his Irish heritage) Michael (for Mac) Gallagher was a beautiful baby. His father spent hours watching him, still not used to the miracle of his creation.

Spring 1972

The city where Finn, Molly, and their one-year-old son settled was in two parts. It was built on the Niagara Escarpment in Ontario, Canada, and had an upper and lower city.

Thomas, Finn's brother, had found them a little house on what was locally known as the "Mountain." Molly was at first intimidated by all the modern conveniences of the house but soon came to love them. Her father had had to work for years for many of these luxuries, but here they were in a modest rental house: a full-size refrigerator, a washing machine and dryer, a full bath, and a powder room.

She was pregnant with their second child, and she and Finn decorated the third small bedroom for a nursery. The array of paint colors, wallpapers, and decorative trims available was dazzling. Everything they could possibly dream of was spread out before them like a buffet. It almost seemed sinful.

She could walk out in the neighborhood to shop, and Finn would drive her on the weekends to "supermarkets" for large items. At first, they would get lost in the many aisles and various nooks.

Finn had immediately gotten a crane operator's job at the steel company and made what they considered to be a great deal of money. At first, he had to work three shifts, but that seemed a small concession for the largesse surrounding them.

He bought a little spaniel to keep Molly company. They named him Daniel. He didn't grow into a large dog, but he could make a tremendous fuss should a stranger cross into his family's territory.

They spent time with Thomas and his wife, Diana, who lived not too far away in a more upscale neighborhood. Thomas was an uptight, humorless man, totally absorbed by his job. He and Finn had long conversations about work and politics, and Molly visited with Diana.

Diana was British, from London, and very unhappy in Canada. She was a medical secretary at a nearby hospital, and, with Thomas, brought in what Finn and Molly considered to be a fortune. Their home was first-rate, but they had no friends to invite over or children to enjoy it.

Diana really didn't have a good word to say about anything. The only times she would become animated were when she talked about England. It got on Molly's nerves, but she would never complain to Finn. As long as he was happy and involved, she was satisfied. She also recognized that, when their new baby arrived, it wouldn't be as easy to get together.

In January 1973, Finn and Molly became parents of a second boy, Dennis Sean. He was utterly lovable from the very beginning. Molly called him her "Baby Bubbles" because he was so cheerful, full of smiles and gurgles.

Patrick, their two-year-old, was a quiet little boy who was happy playing by himself. He considered his baby brother to be mildly interesting, but what he really liked was to sit on his father's lap in his big chair while Finn read aloud to him. The child would sit for hours with Finn's arm around him while Finn read anything – children's stories, the newspaper, history books, the TV Guide – anything. Finn recognized it as odd, but working on the premise that reading is always a good thing, it was a daily ritual.

There was a park near their house, and Finn bought Molly a double stroller. The park was at the edge of the Mountain, and Molly walked there every day and looked down over the lower city.

The city was situated on a large bay. At the east end were the steel plants, belching smoke and dirt, not an appealing neighborhood. But as the city stretched out to the west, its nature changed. There was a central downtown area and residential areas down by the bay and at the foot of the Mountain.

Molly dreamed of a house near the bay. Having lived in Cobh all her life, it was hard being so far from water. She didn't know that Finn felt the same and regularly drove around the streets in the north end after work, looking for a likely property. He wanted to surprise her.

The north end was an old part of the city and had seen better days. Many houses were run down, and many were boarded up. He had in mind a large house which he could bring back to life. There was no rush. He wanted it to be just right in every way.

March of the next year brought Finn and Molly their third son, Gordon Finnigan. Even though he knew it was wrong to have a favorite, Finn loved this child almost as much as he loved Molly.

Gordie looked exactly like his father and was an energetic little boy, “a little dickens” his mother called him. He wasn’t bad, but he was curious and always into something. His older brother Dennis adored him and let him lead him into many misadventures.

Fortunately, Molly was a patient woman having endured life with three older brothers, but sometimes Gordie would have her at her wits’ end. Finn always knew when he got home that his wife had been pushed too far that day, and he always knew who was to blame.

He would call his youngest son before him, and it would go along the lines of, “You’ve upset your mother again, Gordie. You know how that pains me.”

It was hard looking into his own miniature face and scolding the naughty tyke. Gordie would look up, up at his father and say, “I sorry, Daddy.”

Pretty much every time, Finn would pick him up, kiss him, and say, “You know Daddy loves you. I just want you to be a good boy and have a happy life.”

Gordie would feel his father’s strong arms around him and smell his special daddy smell and know that everything was alright and he was in the best place in the world.

Finn and Molly’s plan was to take five years off after Gordie’s birth, move into a new house, and have a couple more children after Gordie started school. Finn asked her if she was sure she wanted any more children after Gordie, and she laughed and said, “Next time, they will be girls.”

On one of his explorations in the north end, Finn met an old lady named Mrs. Callaghan who was from Dublin. They hit it off, and over several visits for cups of tea (and maybe just a titch of Irish whiskey), she told him that her children were becoming insistent that she leave her big old house and move in with one of them. It broke her heart to leave the place where she and her husband had moved when they came from Ireland, and she wondered if Finn would be interested in buying it. That would make her feel better.

Finn was elated. The house was exactly what he'd been looking for. Its condition wasn't too bad. Mrs. Callaghan's children had put a new roof on it several years back and had made sure that the electrical and plumbing systems were safe, although in need of updating. There was lots of cosmetic work needed, but that was no problem for Finn.

As he drove home, he was already planning an extension to the kitchen. There was property for a garden, and a school nearby. He couldn't wait to tell Molly.

When Finn and Molly were invited to meet Mrs. Callaghan's four children, it went extremely well. Mick, her older son, shook Finn's hand vigorously. Like Finn, he worked at the steel company.

The two talked, and Mick said, "Thank God you're Irish. Otherwise, I don't think Mother would have let the house go. I'm sorry we haven't kept it up better, but it's safe while you make upgrades. It's a wonderful house for kids to grow up.

"We know moving away from here will be very traumatic, but we hope to make Mother's remaining time happy. My wife and I have a big house, and I've suggested that she start out living with us. We'll see how that goes and how her health holds. We would all like to share her for a few months at a time. But all that remains to be seen."

"Do you live near the bay," asked Finn. "It's been hard for my wife and me to be away from the water."

"Most of us live nearby because we feel the same way," replied Mick.

Mrs. Callaghan showed her around, and Molly fell in love with the house. "My husband can do anything," she told the old lady. "He will make this house into the Queen of the Street. I hope you will come and visit us lots, if you can handle three little boys, the youngest being especially rambunctious, but sweet-natured."

"I love children," Mrs. Callaghan replied. "It was a great disappointment to us that we only had four. And God bless you for thinking about making time for an old woman."

"I just know that you will become one of our dearest friends," Molly told her warmly and hugged her.

The house was a work in progress. Finn addressed the wiring first. The plumbing could wait. He spent hours sanding and painting. He was anxious to get his family moved in before school started in the fall. Patrick was going into Grade Three and Dennis into Kindergarten.

The kids thought the house was the greatest they had ever seen. In fact, it was. There were endless new games to be played indoors and outside. Hide-and-seek was a big favorite, and Gordie was the champion. More than once, he was hidden for hours, making his mother frantic until she found him curled up, asleep, in some cranny.

Then she realized that she could use Daniel to find him. "Where's Gordie, Daniel? Where's Gordie?" she would ask, clapping her hands. Daniel loved Gordie and could find him easily.

"He's my very best little hound dog," she would say, holding Daniel in her arms and giving him a biscuit.

Work on the house progressed, and the Gallaghers were introduced to the neighborhood by Mrs. Callaghan's family.

They made friends and joined the Irish Club. They didn't see too much of Thomas and Diana, whom Finn called "the human misery," and their world expanded.

In one of his increasingly less frequent talks with his brother, Thomas told him that he was seriously considering moving to England to try to save his marriage. He was concerned about getting work at his age of forty-three. He loved his job at the steel company and didn't want to leave. That was one of the few times Finn had ever seen him show any emotion.

Finn looked at his own wife in the kitchen, singing with the children and talking to Daniel as she baked, her hair tied up and a smudge of flour on one cheek, and his heart glowed. How could one brother be so stiff and unhappy and the other so incredibly blessed?

In May 1978, Finn got a promotion, a really good promotion to a supervisory position. It was well deserved. The bosses considered him to be a gem.

When he was hired, management thought themselves fortunate to have found such an outstanding individual. Not only was he presented by Thomas, who was a valuable senior engineer, Finn had a sterling resume and many positive personal qualities. The feeling was that he would go far after an initial period of proving himself.

The time had come, and Finn was enthusiastic. His reporting group was delighted because everyone liked and respected Finn. He had proven himself as a suitable candidate in every way.

Molly threw him a surprise party in their new home which was really coming along, thanks to Finn's loving work. It turned out to also be a farewell party for Thomas and Diana who were moving back to England.

Finn was truly surprised. It hadn't been easy, but Molly had lots of friends in the neighborhood who helped her keep it a secret. It was a big crowd, people from work, the neighbors, and members of the Irish Club.

Finn was moved as he looked around him. They had come so far in a relatively short time. He knew that he stood on this spot on this day because of the amazing girl who had been presented to him by Fate. *My God,* he thought. And it was almost like a prayer.

Erin and Shannon Gallagher were beautiful little girls with auburn hair and their mother's big brown eyes. Although a year apart in age, they were regularly mistaken for twins. Finn called them his "Irish Roses" and adored them.

Erin had been born after Gordie was safely in Grade One. Shannon followed in eleven months. Their parents were thrilled and considered their days of reproducing to be concluded. "How could we top perfection?" Finn asked with delight.

Their personalities, also identical, were an interesting mix of their parents. They were busy and cheery like Molly. They were also obsessively meticulous about everything they tackled and had a firm sense of right and wrong like Finn.

They loved their mother and father with all their hearts and respected their oldest brother Patrick. He was very serious and liked to talk to them a lot about numbers. Most of it was over their heads, but they were impressed anyway.

Their middle brother Dennis was nice and lots of fun – as long as Gordie wasn't around. They considered Gordie to be little more than a fool, with his constant pranks and teasing. They would gather up their playthings and go to their room if he started pestering them, which was all the time.

By the time the girls were ten and nine, Gordie was so wild and willful that his parents sent him to live in Nova Scotia with Molly's cousins the O'Connors. Finn was alternately angry and heartbroken, which put another black mark beside Gordie's name as far as The Roses were concerned. Life in the Gallagher household improved immensely the minute he walked out the door. And tranquility reigned.

The Roses enjoyed peace such as they had never known in their short lives. Patrick was studying business at university and didn't care about anything else. Dennis was an artist and missed the brilliant colors Gordie brought to their lives. Molly was optimistic as always, but basically she was happy as long as she was with Finn.

Finn felt relieved, but he was also always on edge, waiting for a phone call from Nova Scotia demanding that they take Gordie back. Gradually, he relaxed.

When Gordie came to visit in the summer, he was congenial and cooperative, "like a civilized person," said Finn. The improvements in Gordie's attitude and behavior were, thanks to Molly's cousin Seamus' no-nonsense child-rearing philosophy. He told Finn, "If you've got a bunch of out of control kids, it's like letting the lunatics run the asylum."

The years passed.

Fall 1994

"Will you walk with me, my love? We can look at the sunset."

Molly untied her apron and took his hand. "I will go anywhere you want me to." She still felt the same thrill when he bent down to kiss her. The various children remaining in the kitchen rolled their eyes as they usually did at their parents' displays of affection.

Husband and wife walked down the laneway to the new park on the bay, his arm around her like young lovers. They sat down on a bench beside a large autumnal floral display. Finn looked around somewhat furtively before plucking a purple aster for his bride, and he kissed her.

At that moment, Molly believed that she had never known greater happiness…and the big surprise was still to be presented. “I have something to tell you, Finn. I hope you’ll be happy.”

“What is it, my love?” he asked, looking puzzled.

“I’m carrying our child,” and she moved his hand onto her still-flat belly.

He sat like that silently for a long time. Molly wrapped her arms around his neck. He held her close and told her the thoughts of his heart.

As they rose from the bench to walk home, Finn asked her, “Are you going to give me another little girl to spoil?”

“I’m going to give you anything you want, every day until I die.”

The Campbells

Barbara Elizabeth Murray, June 1, 1938

Nicholas Murray always kept a bottle of first-class single malt scotch whiskey in his office to share with important business associates or good friends, but he never drank alone. Today was an exception.

He was angry and hurt. He felt guilty and vindictive. He was a wealthy and powerful man, but he had no idea what to do. He had just been visited by his daughter Barbara and that Dave, the new mechanic at his Canadian Tire Store. Barbara was smiling and excited as she announced that she was pregnant. Dave was silent.

Nicholas had never liked Dave. He was good-looking in a lounge lizard kind of way, and Nicholas thought he smelled dishonest. He had asked his son Lorne who was general manager of the store why he had hired him and was told that he was a good mechanic and had good references. *Good enough to work on cars,* thought Nicholas, *but not my daughter.*

Sixteen-year-old Barbara was a spoiled brat. Nicholas had to admit that and also admit that it was his fault. She had been born, as a surprise, when her brothers were almost grown up and Nicholas was in his fifties. He was immediately enamored, considering her to be a cherub dropped from heaven. She was her daddy's darling.

Barbara was ten when her mother died. Nicholas didn't think that he could carry on, but the child was his lifeline. He took her everywhere with him, to grown-up places where everyone fussed over her. He gave her everything she asked for and more. He rarely came home, even from work, without a little something for his baby.

But time changed her from a happy, bubbly little girl into a self-absorbed, demanding teenager. The gifts that had pleased her in the past were now seen as her due. She didn't hesitate to tell her father outright what she wanted and to sulk monumentally if it were denied to her.

She got in trouble at school. Although she was bright, she was bored. She had far too much to say and had no fear of reprisal. She was very interested in boys, however, and Nicholas heard a lot of non-specific talk from the teachers at her school and the people in town.

Nicholas was a busy man. With his son Lorne, he owned a third-generation horse farm on the edge of town. He was a smart businessman too. After the war when more and more people were driving cars, he had the foresight to buy a piece of property and build the Canadian Tire Store which was later joined by some other businesses. This was a huge success, drawing lots of traffic, while not hurting the small operations in town. Nicholas was an important member of the town's Chamber of Commerce and had taken a turn as President.

In spite of his wealth and success, he missed his wife and worried about his daughter. Barbara seemed to be growing further and further away from him. He tried to talk to her but was coolly rebuffed. In an effort to please her, he bought her a shiny new car for her sixteenth birthday. The gift was an enormous success, but then he hardly saw her at all. What she was up to, he could only imagine with deep foreboding.

As soon as Barbara laid eyes on the new mechanic at her family's Canadian Tire Store, she knew she must have him. She often dropped by the garage with mysterious car problems. She appeared at the coffee shop where he ate his lunch. She was not subtle.

At closing time one evening, she arrived at the garage and said she needed to talk to him. They moved to the back of the bay, and she slipped off her coat. She was naked underneath, and he took her on the back seat of a car that was waiting for service in the morning.

They began to meet regularly and had hot sex in all kinds of places. Dave knew this wasn't wise, but he couldn't resist a sixteen-year-old who was ready for anything. Barbara was crazy with what she thought must be love.

When, according to her plan, she became pregnant, she coaxed Dave to marry her. They would live in the mansion, and her father and brother would surely give him a major promotion once he was in the family. Dave was smart enough to be skeptical, but he had seen her work her father, and he was sorely tempted. At the very least, he figured, the old man might pay him to get out of town.

Nicholas reacted with quiet rage at the news. He signed the permission document, but before he slid it across his desk, he demanded Barbara surrender her house and car keys. Right then, Dave knew he'd made a big mistake. Now he would be living with a self-centered little bitch in his tiny apartment, no mansion, no elaborate wedding gifts, and no promotion. He'd been had, and he was furious.

Barbara considered it to be merely a small setback. She swore to Dave that her father would relent really soon and they would be back on track with the mansion, etc. It didn't happen.

As her pregnancy advanced, she spent more and more time alone. Dave had resumed his affair with a waitress at a bar on the highway. Sometimes he didn't come home at all. When he did, he was usually drunk and abusive.

Since she didn't go to school anymore, no one saw the bruises or knew of her plight. She was certain that her father would take her back, but her pride stood in the way. She hoped that Dave would turn around when their child was born. He didn't.

Now she was alone with David Murray Johnson. She had no experience with babies but muddled along as best she could. She came to love the little guy and extended herself for him more than she had ever done for anyone before. Dave, who was rarely at home, didn't care one way or another about the baby as long as he was quiet.

Besides drinking heavily and running with women, Dave had a scam going at work. He was turning back odometers for customers who were about to sell their cars. It brought him some additional funds, but it wasn't a shrewd move. He was bound to be caught, and before long, he was.

Dave was sentenced to two years in jail, leaving a pregnant Barbara with her nine-month-old child. She was only a couple of months along, so she took a job waiting tables in the diner under their apartment. Needless to say, she wasn't much of a waitress, but the diner's owner was a third or fourth cousin, so she gave her a chance. On the plus side, Barbara learned that she was able to perform really well when her back was to the wall.

There was a new man in town, opening a John Deere franchise. Michael Campbell was from a John Deere family in New Brunswick. He was an amiable young man and a gentleman.

Nicholas Murray had made his acquaintance and invited him to join the Chamber of Commerce. Michael impressed him as a go-getter, and Nicholas was pleased to help him any way he could with his fledgling business. The future was looking good for Michael Campbell.

Down the street from his store, in the diner where he bought coffee and his lunch, Michael met Barbara. Her waitressing skills had greatly improved, and she had a winning personality when she felt like turning it on. Since tips were important, she was always on her "A" game at work and got on well with the customers.

The regular customers were townsfolk who had known her all her life. They knew her background and the scandals. At first, they thought it was funny to see her brought so low, but soon that was old news and they admired her for coping with her new reality.

Michael Campbell was enchanted. He made a point of coming in for coffee at off hours so he could talk to her. He had heard the stories, and he knew that she was pregnant, but he couldn't stay away. He tried, but he just couldn't resist.

Barbara had changed a lot, and she honestly didn't mean to lead Michael on. But she was lonely, and she enjoyed talking to him, a new person with a different perspective. She didn't realize how he felt about her. She considered herself to be something of a joke in town, her personal business common knowledge, and she was increasingly pregnant, just to ice the cake of her disgrace.

One afternoon, on her day off, she was struggling with the stroller carrying a tired and cranky David up the stairs to her apartment. One of the wheels came off, and she wanted to weep with despair. Michael Campbell came along; it was time for coffee. And he took the matter in hand.

Once inside, she said that she would prepare a thank-you coffee herself if he could wait while she put David down for a nap. Oh, yes, he could, with pleasure.

The world was spinning very fast that afternoon, and Michael made love to her. She had never had such an experience. He used words like "cherish" and "forever," and they were both overcome. It was exhilarating and terrifying, but Michael swore that he would make everything perfect for her and her children. He called them "our children."

And he did. He talked to Barbara's father and asked for his blessing and help. After his initial shock, Nicholas offered both.

The first order of business was to get rid of that Dave. Nicholas' lawyer was engaged to craft a deal too good for Dave to resist. Nicholas offered him more money than he had ever dreamed of.

Dave wasn't interested in Barbara or the children. He would agree to the quickest divorce possible, admitting to adultery and relinquishing all rights to the children. He would never set foot in the town again. Dave considered those conditions to be no problem at all, and he signed the documents with a flourish.

He felt himself the beneficiary of a miracle. He was in such good spirits that he even reflected fondly on the outstanding sex he had enjoyed with Barbara. The annoyance of his marriage to her and the inconvenience of his incarceration seemed like trifles compared to his upcoming happy payday.

The quickest divorce possible in those days took a long time, more than a year. It involved notifications in local newspapers which included details about the marriage, and reasons for its demise. The notifications were to run for six months. It was a humiliating process.

In the meantime, Nicholas invited Barbara and Michael to move to Maple Lane. He figured that there had already been so much disgrace and embarrassment that they should just hold up their heads and enjoy their time together. He had never forgotten his deep sorrow when his wife passed away far too soon, and he believed that the young couple should enjoy their happiness while they could.

And happy they were. Barbara saw the beautiful home through new eyes, a comfortable corner at every turn. It was warm and cozy, and there were no diner smells. She did everything she could to make up to her father for her past selfish and disrespectful behavior, and he was a happy man. He greatly liked Michael and loved his grandson, David Murray. To hell with the town gossip!

Nicholas Michael was born into an adoring family. Barbara and Michael's daughter Emma Lise followed in ten months. She and little Nicholas were like twins, and Barbara nursed them together. Michael called her the Earth Mother. He adored her and thanked God every day that he had found her.

At last they were married, and Michael had a wonderful house built on the river, close to Maple Lane, for their growing family. Two years after Emma came Barbara Katharine, Kathy, and, three years later, Caroline.

Often an ordinary meal seemed like Thanksgiving to Barbara. She would look around the table at serious David, big-hearted Nicholas ever near sweet Emma, bright, busy Kathy, the group leader, the strongest personality, and little Caroline, everyone's pet, her grandpa's "Puppy."

And at the opposite end was her knight in shining armor: her Michael.

If only it could stay like this forever, Barbara thought. Sadly, life's not like that.

In 1973, Nicholas was diagnosed with terminal cancer. Barbara was beside herself, but he was calm and accepting. He told her to try to be happy for him because soon he would see his beloved Elizabeth again. Barbara arranged for him to stay at home with round-the-clock nursing. She spent a great deal of time with him, trying to present as cheerful a face as possible.

At Nicholas' direction, Michael sold their house. Maple Lane and half the farm were part of Barbara's inheritance. The family moved in with mixed emotions.

In November, a member of Michael's family in New Brunswick passed away. Michael asked Barbara to come with him to the funeral, but she couldn't bring herself to leave her father. "Please come home as soon as you can," she begged Michael. "You know I can't bear it when you're not here." He promised to only be away one day and two nights.

In the afternoon after the wake, Michael and his brothers went snowmobiling. There was an accident, and Michael was killed.

Barbara's brother Lorne was the one to deliver the news and help with the funeral arrangements. She was in shock, walking in a fog. Her children surrounded her. She saw their heartbreak, but she wasn't able to do anything but hold on to Caroline who was only eleven years only.

Her elder brother, Nicholas, flew in from Edmonton, bringing along his family. He suggested that his daughter, Shyla, remain behind to help with the children and the care of his father who was shattered by Michael's loss.

In actuality, Nicholas was ridding himself of a problem by foisting it onto Barbara. Shyla was the child of his second marriage, spoiled and out-of-control throughout the course of her nineteen years. She had brought her father and mother endless worries and deep humiliation. From the time she was fourteen, she had slept with any man who paid attention to her. And she usually profited from it. Men loved to give her gifts.

Nicholas and his wife were far beyond their wits' end and didn't know what to do. They actually tried to give her money to go away, but she refused. Why would she leave such an easy situation?

This opportunity, however, was another matter. Living far away from her parents with Barbara, who appeared to be easily manipulated, looked very good indeed. All she had to do was act like a good person until the funeral was over and everyone had cleared out. The old man was well looked after by professionals, so there was nothing for her to do except suit herself.

Shyla was cunning and kept a low profile. Barbara was so distracted she gave her little mind. Nobody remembered the old saying that the devil often disguises himself as a beautiful woman.

In January, the old man died, Barbara at his side. His last words to her were, "Be happy for me. Elizabeth is here," and he smiled. It was the end for Barbara who was sedated and remained in her room for weeks.

Shyla's time had come. She went out late at night to the bars on the highway. Sometimes she didn't come home until dawn, and she stayed in bed until early afternoon.

Basically, the kids had nowhere to turn. Shyla was a force to be reckoned with. Their mother was completely incapacitated, and their uncle Lorne was a weak, self-interested man who couldn't handle any unpleasantness.

By March, Shyla was bored with the local scene. Word was starting to spread about her, and she thought it would be a good time for Barbara and her to go on a vacation. She convinced her father of this during a phone call, and he sent money. He did agree that Barbara could use a break.

It wasn't easy to convince Barbara, who didn't want to leave her room, but Shyla always prevailed, and they headed off to Jamaica for two weeks.

When they arrived at the resort, Barbara was startled to see that everyone was naked. Shyla had neglected to tell her that this was a nudist resort. Barbara hid in their villa while Shyla checked everything out.

Shyla decided that they needed massages to relieve their stress. The masseuse had been coached by Shyla, and he got Barbara quite altered on really delicious drinks called Banana Dreams. Barbara wasn't used to alcohol, and the drinks, especially the drug he had added to them, put her into another dimension.

He gave her a full-body massage and then fucked her royally. As Barbara floated off afterwards, it was Shyla's turn, and she considered the afternoon to be a great success. Lesson learned: a good time was possible as long as Barbara was wasted.

"Wasted" was the operative word. They drank copious amounts of alcohol, smoked ounces of weed, dropped mescaline, and snorted grams of cocaine. They had sex with dozens of men. Everything was cool as long as Barbara never sobered up.

When they got home, they slept for a couple of days. Barbara was horrified when she remembered at least some of what had happened. Shyla soothed her with a few drinks and took her out to the highway. Now the descent to hell had truly begun.

Gossip spread throughout the town. The children were embarrassed at school by the looks and whispers of their classmates. At home, they spent most of their time locked in their rooms since Shyla enjoyed inviting men to visit. It was frightening, and the sights they inadvertently saw were disgusting.

David went to live with his long-time girlfriend's parents. He planned to work the summer at the store, and he was going away to university in the fall. He was counting the days.

The others weren't so lucky, and Kathy applied to a Catholic residential school a couple of hours' drive away for the coming school year. She implored her sisters to come with her. Emma refused to leave Nicholas, and Caroline, who no longer talked, was too scared. Kathy held her in her arms and tried to coax her, but the poor little child just trembled like a frightened poodle.

Nicholas wasn't going anywhere without Emma, so Kathy recognized that she was on her own. She had learned that she could get things accomplished if she woke Barbara up early, talked fast, and shoved pen and paper in front of her.

She was only fourteen but smart and resourceful. She was accepted into Mount Mary Immaculate for Grade Eleven and got a good piece of money for her expenses using her early morning technique.

All the children had to do now was make it through the coming summer. Knowing what was coming, Kathy talked to her uncle Lorne, urging him to call his brother Nicholas and have Shyla removed from the farm. "Oh, I don't want to upset him. He's such a busy man," the coward responded. He was completely intimidated by Shyla.

"How does he run his business?" Kathy asked David. "There must be all kinds of difficult situations all the time."

"He has 'enforcers,'" replied her brother.

As it became summer, things improved slightly when Shyla and Barbara opened the family cottage in Crystal Beach and moved the endless party there. Unfortunately, Shyla had met up with some bikers, so it was a movable orgy.

The four children never rested easy. Many nights they all slept in the same room, sleeping lightly, and waiting for the thunder of motorcycles coming up the lane. Then the big lights in the back by the pool would come on, the music would start blasting, and it was on.

Increasingly, they took refuge on the third floor, one sectioned part of which was accessible through a secret panel, an act of whimsy by their great-great-grandfather. They would cower in the dark, listening to heavy footsteps moving around in the house. They were lucky that, so far, nobody had been together enough to take a good look at the big house and figure out exactly how it was configured.

Sometimes they went to Lorne's house in the early evening to stay overnight. Lorne didn't appreciate the intrusion, but his wife insisted. She was on Kathy's side and wanted to alert the police as to what was going on. Lorne was adamant that no police would ever be called to Maple Lane.

One night at the beginning of September, after Kathy had returned to Mount Mary, Nicholas and Emma were hiding in the dark in the secret room on the third floor. Lorne's wife, Helen, had kept Caroline with them at their house for several nights so, at least, she was safe.

This night was worse than usual. There were more people in the yard and banging about in the house below. A massive bonfire was ablaze out by the pool. The room was lit by the flames.

Nicholas and Emma were terrified. She couldn't stop crying and finally told him about an incident six weeks back.

She and Caroline were taken to the cottage by Barbara and Shyla. They didn't want to go, but Barbara, in a semi-rational moment, insisted that they shouldn't stay at Maple Lane alone.

That having been said, the women went off to a local bar, and two men showed up at the cottage looking for them. Seventeen-year-old Emma was raped. Twelve-year-old Caroline was spared. One of the men, in an unbelievable act of decency, insisted that she was just a little kid and stopped his companion.

Filled with rage and fear, Nicholas held her, kissing her gently. The extraordinary circumstances took them to places they had never been, and later he knew that he had broken the laws of God and man. He was filled with shame and despair and swore to himself that, if they made it through this night, he would put a stop to the nightmare once and for all.

At last, the bonfire dwindled and people began to leave. The noise died down. As the sky lightened, Nicholas and Emma crept downstairs and exited the house through a basement door which was hidden from sight.

They made it to Lorne's house through the wooded area of the property. Lorne and Helen were awake, sitting at the kitchen table. They too had obviously been up all night and looked very much the worse for wear. Caroline had just gone to sleep.

Nicholas took Lorne on immediately. "I'm driving to Edmonton right away. You won't help, and it's obviously no use trying to talk to Uncle Nick on the phone. He's either going to come here immediately and remove that bitch from our lives or I'm going to come back and kill her myself."

Lorne was startled but didn't respond. "Nicky, darling," Helen said. "You're exhausted and at the end of your rope.

You can't drive to Edmonton. It's out of the question." She turned furiously on Lorne.

"Lorne, for once in your fucking life be a man. Call Bill Russell and see if he can fly Nicky out there today. He'll make more of an impact on Nicholas than you will, you useless coward. There's a landing strip on Nicholas' ranch so the trip is straightforward."

Lorne had never heard his wife speak to him like that. However, he could see that the situation was desperate. Bill was a section manager at the store with a pilot's license and his own small plane. Lorne didn't want to involve him in his family business.

"For God's sake, you idiot, everybody from here to Crystal Beach and back knows what is going on. If you won't call him, I will!" Helen was shouting. "And if Bill can't help, I will take Nicky to the airport myself. I'm also calling the Sheriff and Dr. Merrill to get them involved."

Lorne's humiliation at being spoken to like that by his usually mild-manner wife actually stiffened his spine. "I'll call him right now," he said.

"Good. I'm going to the stables to get that gun so it will be at the ready."

Bill Russell came through, and little more than half a dozen hours later they landed on Nicholas' ranch. Nicholas wasn't really surprised to see them, but he hadn't expected an arrival in that fashion.

In the house, young Nicholas minced no words when he told his uncle and his wife in precise detail what had been happening since they had dumped their daughter at Maple Lane after Michael Campbell's funeral.

Nicholas knew it was all his fault and stared at the kitchen floor. His wife, who had never supported the idea of leaving

Shyla at Maple Lane, told him angrily, "You have to go there now. You are to blame, and you must make it right!" She said to her nephew, "Nicky, I've never felt such shame. I beg your forgiveness. Please stay here with me while your uncle handles this situation."

Nicky collapsed in a chair and burst into tears.

It was very late when Bill Russell landed at the airstrip outside town. Nicholas had phoned Lorne from Edmonton before they left and told him to be there when they arrived. They headed for Maple Lane which was quiet and in darkness.

The brothers crept upstairs and found Shyla passed out on her bed. Nicholas shook her awake and demanded to know where Barbara was. Shyla was so groggy and amazed at seeing her father that she told them. Nicholas furiously told her to get her things together because he was coming back for her.

Before they left the house, Nicholas called the doctor to alert him that they would be at his office soon and Neil, the sheriff, their lifelong friend, was to arrange where to meet them. At a sleazy motel on the highway, admitted to one of the rooms by the night manager, they rescued their sister from a scene of such degradation that Nicholas was never able to burn it from his memory.

They took her to Dr. Merrill who checked her over, deeming her condition to be very serious, and then they took her in Lorne's van to a rehabilitation facility about fifty miles away.

After she was admitted, they returned to the farm. Another day was dawning, and Shyla had flown, taking one of the cars.

Nicholas sternly told his younger brother to see to the damage to the house and grounds. He advised that he put an electric fence across the front and a locked gate on the entrance to the long lane. He said to get a couple of trained guard dogs.

Lorne finally recognized the seriousness of the situation he had allowed to fester for so long. His wife never looked him in the same way again.

The two girls stayed with Lorne and Helen. David and Kathy were away at school. Nicholas remained on his uncle's ranch. He didn't return to Maple Lane for more than thirty years. Shyla was gone, just plain gone, no one knew where.

Satan had lived at Maple Lane since Michael Campbell's death in November 1973 until September 1974. No one in the family would ever be the same.

Barbara came home after nine months. She was like a stranger. David unenthusiastically returned to stay in the house until school began in the fall. Kathy had taken a summer job at Mount Mary and only came back for a couple of days to see her sisters. She could scarcely bring herself to look at Barbara. She blamed her mother for everything.

Caroline had bonded with Helen, who called her "my baby," and she clung to her obsessively. Emma returned to the big house. She was seeing the same psychiatrist that Barbara visited every two weeks.

She did not reveal her secrets. The doctor knew she was holding back but persisted in trying to get her to open up. He prescribed her an antidepressant which didn't help. She seemed to be caught in an endless loop in her head. Sometimes she didn't know where she was or how she had come to be there. When she walked, she felt like there were giant springs attached to her feet. Unlike Caroline, she never cried.

At the beginning of September, David went back to university. His girlfriend drove, and Barbara went too. Her doctor had advised her to get out of the house if she had a chance.

It was a blazing hot afternoon. Emma was in the kitchen and turned on the cold water in the large, deep utility sink. She was wearing a long, flowing skirt and a tank top. Dreamily, she removed her top and began to sponge herself. She could feel the water. It felt good.

Suddenly, she became aware of someone else in the room. It was Jimmy Sheehan, a not-really friend of David's. He was a rough young man from a trashy family, but he and Dave liked to work on cars together sometimes.

Jimmy was staring at Emma in awe. "My God, Em," he said, "I never realized you were so beautiful." He approached her and gently dried her with a towel. "You're like one of the foreign statues in books," he said inarticulately, and he kissed her. She did not resist; she didn't make a sound. In fact, she put her arms up around his neck.

After he was gone, she thought that she had dreamt it.

Months passed, and Barbara seemed a little stronger although she was sleep-deprived. She couldn't sleep at night because she would see Michael, just a short distance away. No matter how she ran to catch up, she could never reach him. She always woke up in tears.

She mourned her father and grieved endlessly about the misery she had brought to her children. She had constant flashes of things that had happened, horrible things that she had done. The shame she suffered made her suicidal much of the time.

She loved all her children, but Emma Lise had always been her favorite, the first baby she and Michael had conceived. To see the human wreckage she was now was a bitter pill.

One day she was looking at Emma standing in the kitchen and she realized that the girl was pregnant. She seemed to be totally unaware. With the psychiatrist's help, Emma vaguely remembered her encounter with Jimmy Sheehan.

Barbara knew that Jimmy wasn't a great choice for a mate, but, in her muddled mind, she thought it might help Emma to have a husband and child. She was projecting her sorrow over what she had lost onto the badly damaged girl.

Jimmy Sheehan's family was delighted to have their son marry into the Murray/Campbell fortune. Jimmy didn't want to get married, but his formidable mother was in charge.

When Kathy heard what had happened, she was outraged. David, who knew Jimmy well, was horrified. Their distress was warranted. Emma and Jimmy lived with his large family, and it was hell on earth for the poor broken girl. She was a helpless prisoner.

Their first child, Billy, was born two months later. Ten months afterwards, Jimmy Jr. was born. In another month or so, Emma was pregnant again. Jimmy was unhappy and drank and beat her. His mother worked her like Cinderella. They kept her from her family, which wasn't difficult, Barbara being extremely reclusive and the children having fled Maple Lane.

On a very unusual day, Barbara ventured out and decided to stop by the Sheehans' to see Emma and her babies. Fortunately, Mother Sheehan had gone shopping, and Emma was alone. She was far along in her third pregnancy and had a black eye from that morning's beating. She looked at her mother as if she didn't know her.

Barbara got her daughter and the babies into her car and hurried home. She activated the electric gate and called the family lawyer. It seemed that she still had the ability to pull it together when her back was to the wall. She mustered the strength to get through this crisis, but not without more damage to her own self-esteem and to Emma. Everywhere she looked, she saw accusing eyes.

David was graduated with a Bachelor of Finance. He took over the Canadian Tire Store and married his long-time girlfriend.

Lorne retired to Victoria, and his wife left him. His oldest son, Todd, who was a vet, took over Lorne's half of Maple Lane Farms. He was a nice guy who knew something, but nowhere close to all, about what had happened. Finally, a good, normal person was introduced to the family mix.

Kathy graduated from Mount Mary Immaculate with the highest honors and earned a scholarship to the University of Toronto. She swore she would never return to Maple Lane.

Young Nicholas stayed on his uncle's ranch and graduated from a program in agricultural equipment maintenance and repair at a local community college. His relationship with his uncle was strained, but his aunt became the mother he had lost. Ultimately, he married a local girl and they set up a home on the ranch. He was a valuable asset to his uncle's operation.

He did not communicate with anyone at Maple Lane although his heart ached for Emma. His distance was sort of a pact he had made with God.

Caroline grew up troubled and deeply depressed, particularly after her Aunt Helen moved away. When she was sixteen, she ran away to Toronto. At the bus station, on arrival, she met a young man who was playing guitar on the street

He too was a runaway from Kingston and Queen's University. He was positive he could be a success making music, a long and hungry road pursued by many other displaced young people.

He loved Caroline at first sight. He had been attracted to her sad eyes, and he wanted to save her. Instead, after they wandered like nomads through the lanes and alleyways and the crash pads of what had been hippy Yorkville, he made her pregnant. No miracle presented itself in the first few months, and the young couple had no choice but to go to Maple Lane.

Barbara was happier than she was able to express to see her daughter. Marc was a fine young man from a good family, and she was glad to have them at home. Extremely glad, in fact. Caroline was her baby, not Helen's, and Barbara was anxious to help.

On December 28, 1978, the child was born. Her name was Theresa Katharine.

After much discussion, in early 1979, Marc resolved to travel to Kingston and reconcile with his parents. He was prepared to return to Queen's in the fall if they would take him and Caroline and their baby into their lives. He left on the bus, full of optimism. He promised to phone as soon as he reached Kingston, but the call never came.

Caroline was frantic. Barbara called the Toronto police, wondering if, on his stopover in that city, he had gotten into trouble. The police didn't laugh, but they might as well have. At that time, hundreds of parents from all over Canada were trying to find their runaway progeny in the big city.

Soon Caroline couldn't wait anymore. She set out to look for Marc herself. She found him, but nobody ever knew the details. One night in fall, she was picked up by the police, wandering barefoot in the street. She was pregnant, but unable to say where she'd been or where Marc might be.

She was returned to Maple Lane and bore her child in December. She wrote Marc's name on the birth certificate, but she never spoke of him again or what had happened between them. He was never found, and Caroline never came back to the real world.

Katherine Campbell, December 28, 1959
Edward Claude Gascoyne, December 2, 1952

February 1984

Eddie hadn't come home until 5 a.m. He had an important meeting at 10, and Katherine was even more worried than usual.

He had been devolving at an increasingly rapid rate, even faster than the pace he had been keeping for the last two years.

She tried to shake him awake, but he was out cold. She picked out a suit and shirt and tie for him to wear, and she paced nervously. At eight-thirty, she put an icy-cold face cloth on the back of his neck, and he came around, fighting.

"What the fuck, you bitch," he bellowed.

"Baby," she said in a quiet, reasonable voice, "you have to get ready for the Kinoshita meeting at ten. I've got your clothes laid out, but you'd better get cleaned up now."

"*Mon dieu,*" he yelled, "how could I possibly manage without a nagging, fucking cunt on my back?" But he did get up and headed to the shower. She heard the water running and him swearing in two languages. She was trembling.

When he emerged, he looked terrible. He got partially dressed and went to the dining room table. He laid out a line and snorted it. Katherine knew better than to say anything, but he saw the expression on her face.

"Is there something you'd like to say to me, *mon amour*?" and he grabbed her tightly by her shoulders.

"Of course not, Eddie," she said evenly. "You know what you're doing."

In spite of her effort to placate him, he didn't like her tone and backhanded an unfortunate lamp, which happened to be nearby.

"I have to go," she backed away and headed quickly for the foyer. She grabbed her purse and got out of the apartment. She was so frightened that she didn't wait for the elevator and ran to the stairs. She could still hear him crashing about, cursing loudly.

It was time to put her plan into action. She would return to the apartment after he was gone – she knew full well that he would go to the meeting – and get the suitcases she had been secretly packing. It was time to leave.

She would not bring her child into this world. "Oh, Eddie," she whispered as she choked back a sob.

Katherine had nowhere to go but the farm. She had never taken Eddie there and had always been vague whenever she spoke of it. She called it "The House of the Living Dead." She hoped that at such time as he ever got straight he wouldn't remember anything she had said.

It took her two days to get there. She flew from Vancouver to Chicago, took the Amtrak to Buffalo, flew to Toronto, and got a limo to the farm. Fortunately, she had plenty of money from freelance interior design work she had done, and Eddie had always been generous.

Her mother was unexpectedly welcoming and even expressed sympathy on hearing what had happened. Delicate Emma hugged her and looked dismayed at seeing her strong sister in such a dreadful state.

The first while was awful. Katherine cried endlessly. Her mother listened outside her bedroom door at night, but it had been so long since she had made an effort for anyone she didn't know what to do. Emma crept downstairs from her third floor hideaway and came in to hold her sister in her arms. She worried for the baby, Katherine being so overwrought. “Eddie, oh, Eddie,” she sobbed.

Her little niece Theresa would curl up on her lap, cuddling against the baby. Somehow, this brought the most comfort of all.

In the summer, her child arrived, a healthy boy with his father’s powerful lungs, black, black eyes and long dark lashes. Katherine said he batted his eyes at her from the time he was born. She named him Edward Claude Gascoyne.

August 1985

Time passed, as it must, and Eddie grew into a beautiful, charming little boy. “Charming” described him to a tee. He knew exactly how to play his audience. With a couple of bats of his father’s eyes and his perfect face upturned for a kiss, he won the hearts of all who met him. His mother was helpless before him.

As his first birthday approached, she taught him a game: “*Quel age as-tu, Eddie?*” she would ask. Coyly, he would raise one finger, bat his eyes, and lift his face for kisses, in the French style, one on each check. Then Katharine would clap her hands and the baby would do the same.

This game was so adorable that his relatives played it endlessly with him, even his rugged Sheehan boy cousins, ages nine, eight, and seven. When his mother would relinquish him from her arms, some other enchanted fool would pick him up. His grandmother wondered if the child would ever walk or would be carried through life. Although captivated herself, she worried about him to the best of her limited ability.

The day before his birthday, Katherine knelt beside him as he splashed cheerfully in a small plastic pool in front of the house. He and she kept up a steady dialog while his cousins Theresa and Sharon played with kittens on the veranda. It was a beautiful day with a flawless sky, and Katherine regarded her son with love so profound that she could think of nothing else.

"Someone's coming," Sharon observed. Sure enough, a car was making its way through the maple tunnel toward the house. Visitors were not usual, and Katherine stood up and gathered her baby into a big towel. The little girls, their arms full of kittens, joined her.

The car pulled into the parking area, the door opened, and the driver emerged. It was Eddie.

He looked fit and tanned as he moved with his trademark laid-back stroll toward the group. About five yards away, he removed his sunglasses. "*Bonjour,*" he said in his familiar Eddie voice, "I am Gascoyne."

Katherine thought she would certainly faint dead away. That was the first thing he had said to her when he approached her in Winnipeg. "*Moi aussi,*" she responded, and he smiled.

He moved closer. "Girls, this is my husband, Eddie. Eddie, these are my nieces Theresa and Sharon and their kittens."

Eddie bowed slightly and said, "Ladies, kittens, it is my pleasure." The girls' eyes were big as saucers.

"You're gorgeous," blurted out Theresa. Kathy laughed, and Eddie smiled, his aw-shucks-Eddie-smile.

"You warm my heart, Theresa."

"Why don't you go out back and make sure no one is killing anyone," Katherine suggested. "And leave the kittens on the porch with their mother in case the boys want to use them for lacrosse balls again." They did as they were told, with a number of backward glances.

He stood right in front of her now. "And who is this?" he asked, looking at Eddie.

"This is your son. His name is Edward Claude Gascoyne, and he will be one year old tomorrow."

Katherine had never known Eddie to be speechless. She was sorry that she hadn't broken the news more gently. "Want to see something neat?" she asked him.

"Sure."

"Come sit with me on the steps," she invited. They sat down, and she held the baby on her knee. "*Quel age as-tu, Eddie*?" she asked the child. Up went one finger. Two eye bats, and his little face raised for kisses. "*Bonne fete,* my angel," she congratulated him. He beamed and clapped his little hands.

"Do you want to play too?" she asked her husband.

"I don't think I can," he responded slowly in a most un-Eddie-like voice.

"Would you like to hold him?" she inquired.

"Okay." And he took him from her.

The baby couldn't take his eyes off Eddie. He wasn't particularly familiar with men, but he seemed to intuit that there was something special about this person. He sat happily on his father's lap and pleasantly poked at his face. He seriously wanted to play with the sunglasses which hung from the neck of Eddie's shirt.

"This is why you left me," Eddie said.

"I kept hoping my Eddie would come back," Katherine told him. "But when I found out I was pregnant, I had to go. It broke my heart," she said simply.

"That's all in the past, my love," he said. "I promise you."

"Come upstairs with me while I put Eddie down for a nap. Then we can talk about everything."

Katherine sat on a love seat, her child cradled in her left arm. She nursed him, talking softly to him about all the wonderful things that had happened that morning. The little guy was sleepy after the fresh air and excitement, and his eyelids were heavy. Pictures of his mommy and the kittens and the brown person with the shiny toy passed through his head. Soon he was in dreamland.

Eddie sat on Katherine's right. As she tended to their son, he lowered his face to her shoulder. "*Ma femme. Mon amour*," he whispered. Katherine knew he was crying, but she would never let on. Gascoyne men didn't cry. She gave him a minute and then rose to put the baby in his crib.

She turned to her husband. "And now it's just us," she said. "Please tell me what has happened to you," and she sat beside him.

He took a deep breath and began. "I went to the Kinoshita meeting. I was completely out of control, and Larry tried to keep me from going into the conference room. He said he would tell them I had the flu, and he would carry the ball. I refused.

"I'll spare you the details of my behavior, but after about five minutes, Larry asked if we could break briefly and got me out of the room. He said we needed to speak privately and took me into a stairwell. The meeting was on the mezzanine of the Embassy, so the stairs at that level go directly to the parking garage.

"He got me about half-way down, as you can imagine I was protesting vigorously, when we rounded a corner where his driver Marc, you know, the huge guy, and Pete Rowntree were waiting. Baby, they strong-armed me down the rest of the way into a limo that was waiting at the door to the stairs. They literally kidnapped me. Although I was really coked up, I couldn't fight them.

"I tell you this: if things had gone wrong, those guys would be in prison now and I would be dead or, at the very least, living on the street, I owe Larry Villeneuve my life, and I will never forget."

"My God, Eddie," Katherine clutched his hand. It seemed a miracle that he was here beside her at this moment.

"Larry went back into the meeting and said that I had been sick and taking medication…you know. Of course they didn't believe it, but it was the best he could do. Naturally, by lunch, everyone in town was talking about Eddie Gascoyne's meltdown.

"I didn't know it, but Larry had been in contact with a rehab facility for a couple of months. He told them he didn't know exactly when it would happen, but he would get me there when it did. They were waiting for me, and sent me to detox for two weeks. Then I was in the program for four months."

"How did Larry know it would happen that day?" she asked.

"You knew, didn't you?"

"Pretty much. I had never seen you that bad. I was really scared."

"Well, Larry was the one who brought me home at five o'clock that morning, and he knew."

"Oh, my God, baby. What was it like in rehab?"

"Actually, it was good. It was undoubtedly the best thing that had ever happened to me – besides meeting you, of course."

"Of course."

"The place was first-class, up in Squamish. Beautiful grounds and scenery. I met with a counsellor each day, and we talked about my issues, specifically why I am so driven. When I came to a better understanding of myself and my family dynamics, I understood that I must try to slow down and relax.

That sounds obvious and simple, but it's not. I've had to work very hard.

"Slowing down didn't mean lounging around, feeling sorry for myself. It meant diverting my attention from my addiction – and I don't mean cocaine. I mean my lust for success, more and more success. I could never get enough."

"What did you do?" Katherine asked.

"I kept journals about my activities and my feelings. I wrote you letters even though I had no idea where you were. I got into gardening."

"Gardening?"

"Yep. I really enjoy it. I love being outside. I love seeing nature doing its work.

"And I took cooking classes. I figured that I had owned restaurants and probably would again so maybe I should know something about cooking. I like the way that, I as a novice, have to focus and follow recipes precisely. My mother could cook a six-course meal for thirty dead drunk, but she has the knowledge and experience. For me, this has been a lesson in taking things slowly and deliberately.

"As we progressed in the course, sometimes the instructor would put something wrong into the recipe which made the exercise more interesting. Our experience should tell us that it was incorrect, but we had to have the confidence to question or correct it."

"Eddie," she laughed. "I never dreamed I would hear you talk like this. I'm so impressed! What else did you do?"

"I exercised, walked and biked, ate, and slept great. But I yearned for you, my beloved girl. Please tell me how it was for you."

The horrible time came flooding back. "After I got here, I cried for five months until Eddie was born. My mother was amazingly kind, and Emma was so worried. Theresa was my best little friend, and she spent a lot of time talking to Eddie in my belly.

"When he was born, I couldn't believe the miracle he was, just like you. For a long time, I wouldn't let him out of my arms, but I gradually got better and trusted that no one would take him away from me. And now he's almost one, and you're here, and I just keep pinching myself. You really are here, aren't you?"

"You tell me," and he kissed her, gently, deeply, passionately.

"Yes," she said.

"Gran, Gran, Eddie's here," Theresa reported excitedly. Barbara was confused. Then it clicked. "Do you mean 'Eddie, oh, Eddie'?" she asked.

"Yes."

"Well, well. Where are they now?"

"Upstairs, I guess. It's the baby's nap time."

"I think I'll have a coffee, that being the case," Barbara said. "I don't want to miss anything. Did you see him and talk to him?"

"Yes. He's gorgeous! And really nice."

"Hmm. How was Kathy?" Barbara inquired.

"She was fine, and she called him 'my husband.'"

"It should be an interesting dinner, my little lamb."

It was obvious to Barbara that the consummation of their reunion had been triumphant. Kathy and Eddie came into the den, Eddie carrying their child on one arm, the other draped around Katherine's shoulders in casual possession. He was indeed "gorgeous," a big man with black hair and black eyes that he had passed on to his son. He smiled at her, a warm, inclusive smile, his white teeth gleaming in his tanned face.

My God, she thought, *what are you going to do about a man like that?* She sighed.

"Mother," Kathy said, "This is my Eddie." She looked like a bride, shining. She had even put on a pretty summer dress and the gold hoop earrings Barbara knew Eddie had given her for their first anniversary. As for Eddie, Barbara thought that if he were a peacock, he would be in full display. Their pure joy was outrageous.

"I'm glad you're here, Eddie," Barbara said. "It's been a long unhappy time without you."

"Why don't you let Kathy give the baby his dinner now so we can relax and enjoy ours? Sit with me and have a drink." It was not an invitation.

"Scotch and water, ma'am," he responded, handing Eddie off to his wife.

They settled in. "Am I to assume you have conquered your demons?" she asked outright.

"I've come to understand what I am up against, and it's not cocaine. It's the force inside me that pushes me to win, endlessly win. It's not a competitive drive, just the need to secure the prize. No success is enough to satisfy the hunger.

"I spent more than four months in rehab with intensive psychotherapy. I learned a lot about myself and something about how to fight the demon. Cocaine was a means to an end, that is, a tool to help me work twenty-two-hour days, three hundred and sixty-five days a year. Sadly, the tool became the master."

"Are you done with it? Has it cost you enough?"

Eddie put his hands over his face. When he lowered them, the mask was gone.

"Barbara," he said, "my wife left me. I didn't know where she had gone or if she would ever come back. Today I met the son I didn't know I had. I missed the first year of his life. I lost millions of dollars and almost all my credibility. Only due to the loyalty of a few friends am I in a position to be working my way back.

"However, thanks to cocaine, I got help for my deep-seated problem, and I am trying very hard to not let that demon destroy me. When I came here today, I was looking for Katherine. I didn't think she would actually be here. Of course, I didn't know about Eddie.

"This has been the most remarkable day of my life. Nothing will take them away from me. Can you understand me?"

"More than you know," Barbara said. "I'm going to believe you and offer you any help I can give. I have a bevy of personal issues, but I have managed to leave cocaine behind for almost ten years so far, anyway.

"Come on, let's go and see our children in the kitchen."

Dinner was the most fun it had ever been. The boys immediately took to Eddie and had endless questions for him. Eddie was in an excellent mood, and he was used to children, so he had jokes and tricks that had the boys howling with laughter. Even serious Emma laughed and smiled. It did her mother's heart good.

Later, when they were alone, Eddie commented to Katherine that he had never seen such a sad household. The following day was their baby's first birthday, and Eddie suggested that they have a wonderful party that would cheer everyone up. He had always been his family's entertainment coordinator, so he knew he could pull it together easily. He also said that they should have a games tournament on the day before he, Katherine, and Eddie left to go home.

Katherine was always turned on by Eddie's energy and agreed to help. She knew that he would have the whole thing planned by breakfast.

A quick trip to town in the morning brought home banners, hats, a piñata, and everything for an ice cream sundae bar. A few other family members joined the group, and the baby's first birthday was celebrated in fine style. Marta, the housekeeper, had made a big cake and young Eddie was the center of attention to his delight. Many games of "Bonne Fête" were enjoyed by all.

Next morning, the First Annual Maple Lane Farms Triathlon was held for the boys. It comprised two laps in the pool, a foot race to Cousin Todd's house about a quarter-mile away and a return-bicycle race. Young Brian was the surprise winner after Billy, the favorite, crashed his bike trying to run his brother off the road.

The Chinese checkers tournament was more subdued but still lots of fun for everybody, the winner being Emma. She was so pleased you'd think she'd won the lottery.

The special closing event was the doll/kitten fashion show presented by Theresa and Sharon. Eddie was the Master of Ceremonies. The girls had made a big cardboard box into a stage on which they posed their dressed up dolls. The piece de resistance was when they brought out their kittens, also resplendent in doll clothes and bonnets.

The first minute went well, with oohs and aaws from the audience, but then the kittens freaked out and ran amok, biting at their finery and trying to get their hats off. They knocked over the dolls and tried to make a break for it. It was chaos, drawing boos and jeers from the boys and hysterical laughter from the adults.

The kittens were captured, undressed, and petted into calmness. Eddie, not sure what to do, called the contest a draw: Pumpkin Cat, Theresa's favorite, was named The Best Personality. Miss Mew, Sharon's cat, was named The Meanest. Both girls were satisfied and took the trophy upstairs to display in their bedroom.

"*Mon dieu,*" said Eddie as he collapsed in a chair. Marta handed him a beer. Barbara, wiping tears from her eyes, said, "Eddie, I don't think I've ever laughed so hard in my life."

"Come on," Billy called. "Let's go swimming!" And so they did before enjoying a great barbeque supper.

The next morning was gray to suit the general mood. The endlessly macho Billy was near tears as he begged Eddie not to go. Eddie looked at the array of sad faces and spoke with his characteristic enthusiasm.

"Listen, everyone," Eddie said, "Kat and I have decided to come back at Christmas to be here for the holidays and Kat and Theresa's birthday on the 28th. But we want you to do something for us: Kat would like you to hold a Christmas Eve Open House like you did in the old days before your husband died, Barbara."

"Well, I suppose I could do that," Barbara said hesitantly. "They were really nice occasions. But I would need everyone to pitch in and help me." There was vigorous agreement.

"Okay," Katharine said. "We will try to fly in on the 23rd so we can help too."

And so the wheel turned round.

December 28, 1994

Billy Sheehan loved his cousin Theresa. They had grown up together, and she had always made him feel funny in a way he couldn't describe. By the time he was seventeen and she was thirteen, he was able to be specific. She was his, and he loved her.

Their time together as secret lovers was about to end, at least temporarily. Billy was going away after the New Year. He couldn't stand life on the farm any more.

Theresa and Sharon were moving to the city with their mother who was, for the moment anyway, in good enough shape to care for them. There was a lot of skepticism within the family as to the potential success of this venture, but Barbara felt she should at least give her daughter a chance. The move also meant that Theresa could attend a prestigious private school and Sharon a first-class high school.

In the early morning hours of her sixteenth birthday, Billy snuck into Theresa's room to say a private goodbye. He said he would be back in six months. He promised her the future, and she believed him. "Don't leave me alone too long, Billy," she said.

The Gallaghers and the Campbells

Gordon Finnegan Gallagher, March 19, 1974

Theresa Katharine Campbell, December 28, 1978

May 21, 1995

"What are your parents like?" Theresa asked him.

"Who really knows?" Gordie replied. "They are so obsessed with each other it's like the rest of us aren't even there. Except, of course, for the baby, the miraculous child of their old age."

"How old is the baby?"

"She's brand new, born on April Fool's Day, and her name is Mary Frances." Gordie was smart enough to realize that he needed to soften his tone in order to not sound jealous or petty, particularly since the tiny pink morsel at home wasn't really the cause of his bitterness.

Although Gordie was their third child, Finn had assisted in the birth. He was profoundly moved by the experience. He stayed with Molly while she slept, exhausted, and cradled the baby until he wanted to nurse. Finn told Molly that those twenty-four hours changed his life. He believed in God. His happiness was boundless; his love for his wife and baby son were like an ache in his chest. He believed in a happy future.

Gordie was the image of Finn: handsome, tall, and slim with dark hair and piercing blue eyes. He was mischievous, bright and capable but without focus. For the first few years of his life, he followed Finn like a dog. As he got older, Finn tried to teach him things, but his slap-dash approach to projects made his father lose patience. Finn expected nothing less than perfection from himself and everyone else.

Time passed and Gordie had had enough of hearing "Think it through" and "Focus, for Christ's sake." He discovered girls – or they discovered him. The endless phone calls to the house led Finn to try to caution the boy; he was deeply worried for him.

By the time he was sixteen, Gordie was wild and wilful. Finn sent him to Nova Scotia to stay with Molly's cousins.

He lived there for five years, finishing high school and his Auto Mechanic certification. He cut a swath through the local girls, breaking hearts, but he somehow remembered his father's warnings. As the years passed and no bad news arrived on their doorstep, Finn said to Molly, somewhat grudgingly but mainly with relief, "Thank God the boy's got some common sense after all."

Gordie had only just returned to town a few weeks before. He was living with his parents, and he had a job at an auto repair shop. He and Finn stayed out of each other's way. This upset Molly because, in spite of the calm and in-control manner which defined Finn to those who didn't know him as she did, she knew he was hurt by the situation but didn't know how to fix it.

This year, it was an unusually warm spring. On Saturday of the May 24 weekend, Gordie was invited to visit with a couple of his friends. He had no intention of spending the day around his father and readily agreed.

Soon after he arrived and had a beer in his hand, there was a knock at the back gate. Being closest, Gordie opened the gate and literally stammered a greeting to the prettiest girl he had ever seen. “I’m Theresa,” she laughed. “May I come in?”

Gordie made a quick recovery and brought her into the yard. The four young people socialized under a large umbrella. Gordie could hardly take his eyes off Theresa nor she him.

Theresa thought, *He’s so incredibly good-looking. How could I possibly be of interest to him?*

Gordie thought, *I’m going to marry this girl.*

In a while, their friends went into the house, and the smitten pair began to talk. They talked for many hours, into dusk, telling the stories of their lives and the lives of those close to them. Gordie knew that he had to be with her, no matter what the cost. Theresa knew that she would never willingly leave his side.

Once it was dark, Gordie walked Theresa home. No one from her dysfunctional family unit was there; everyone had gone to her grandmother’s farm for the holiday weekend.

When they entered the apartment, Gordie, who had not so much as touched Theresa’s hand during their hours-long conversation, said to her, “Please show me where you sleep.”

She led him to the bedroom and showed him the bed that was hers. “Why do you care?” she asked.

“Because, when I’m not with you, I want to be able to imagine where you are.”

He took her in his arms and kissed her deeply.

“Do you understand that you’re going to be my wife?”

“Yes.”

“Are you on birth control?”

"No."

"Do you care what happens?"

"No. Do you?"

"No."

And so they didn't care all night long.

Gordie got home as the sunrise was a sliver on the horizon. He didn't want his mother to know that he had spent the night with the girl he was going to bring home for family dinner that afternoon.

He didn't feel tired. He was exhilarated by the amazing twist of fate. He wasn't even irritated by the fact that Finn was sitting in the living room with his baby daughter in his arms.

"Good morning, Daddy," he said quietly. "Why are you up so early?"

"The baby was a bit fussy, so I brought her down here to let your mother rest a little more."

Gordie sat down beside his father and gave the baby his finger to hold. She seemed to look right back at him and smiled. "She smiled at me, didn't she?"

"I think she knows you, son. I've come to believe she knows many things."

"It's not like you to be mystical, Daddy. Aren't you just being Irish?"

"The world has become more mystical, Gordie. How could I imagine I would have an infant daughter in my fifties?"

And then Gordie said the most loving thing he had said to his father since he was a boy: "You're a great father," and touched Finn's hand. "See you in a while. I'm going to sleep a bit now. I'm bringing someone to dinner today."

This had never happened before, but Finn maintained a neutral expression.

"See you later," he said. "And by the way, you smell lovely." Theresa's smell was all over him.

"I've been trying a new cologne. Seems to be working pretty good," and he bounded up the stairs two at a time

"What's going to happen next, my little angel?" Finn whispered to Mary Frances.

That afternoon when Gordie brought Theresa home for Sunday dinner, he thought he would burst with pride. His parents liked her right off. They let her hold Mary Frances. His brothers were jealous. His sisters wanted to know where she had bought the little dress she was wearing and the adorable earrings that matched it. Gordie considered it to be a winning occasion.

When they were leaving, Gordie, his arm around Theresa, blithely announced that they were going to get married. After a startled silence around the table, Molly inquired cheerily, "And when will that be, dears?"

"Next week, I hope," said foolish Gordie. It got worse. "We're going to see her grandmother tomorrow to get her permission because Theresa is only sixteen," he added like a complete idiot. Finn leaned forward, his hand shielding his eyes.

The silence could be cut with a knife. "Well, please don't do anything without letting us know first," Molly said pleasantly.

"Okay, Mommy. See you later, everyone." And so was Theresa introduced to the Gallaghers.

It was customary for the sisters to help Molly clean up after meals and do the dishes. This time, Molly suggested that all the children go about their business and enjoy what was left of the beautiful day. She and Finn would do the chores.

When they were alone, Finn exploded. “How in the hell did we get that boy?”

“You know perfectly well how we got him. And we love him. He’s just impulsive and not very well grounded,” Molly told her husband soothingly.

“We tried our best, Molly. What could we have done differently?”

“There’s no point in that, Finn. All we can do is hope that the grandmother has some common sense. As an aside, I might mention that I was fifteen when you married me, and that turned out quite well, don’t you think?”

“The characters in this piece are completely different, and you know it.”

“Gordie is twenty-one, and there is nothing we can do but hope for the best. He does have a job,” and she smiled sweetly at her husband.

“God, give us strength,” Finn replied.

In the car, Gordie took Theresa’s face in his hands and kissed her over and over. “I wanted to do this the whole time we were in the house,” he said.

“Do you think you should have told them that we’re getting married?” Theresa asked.

“Well, we are, aren’t we?” Gordie looked genuinely concerned.

“Yes, but Gran might not agree right away,” Theresa said. “She is pretty cranky and doesn’t like people much.”

“I’ll make sure she likes me,” Gordie promised. “If she says no, we’ll be engaged until we can make it happen.”

“I love you, Gordie,” she said.

“You’re my girl,” he said and kissed her again.

It was shortly after noon when Gordie and Theresa arrived at Maple Lane Farms. He was somewhat intimidated by the magnificent house and park-like grounds

Theresa had explained that her grandmother drank pretty steadily from noon onwards, so it was best to approach her early. She said that she held her liquor well, not getting especially drunk until late at night. "Just don't let her smell fear" was Theresa's advice, only half joking.

Barbara was in the den with her best friend Kim Scott who, Theresa was surprised to see, looked pregnant and was drinking orange juice instead of scotch as was Barbara. Kim left the three alone.

"Gran, this is my boyfriend, Gordie Gallagher. We want to talk to you."

Barbara noted how very handsome Gordie was and could foresee no good on the horizon. "Talk," she said.

"Mrs. Campbell, I have only just met Theresa, but I know we are meant to be together forever. We want your permission to marry," Gordie declared fairly smoothly.

"You are aware that Theresa is sixteen years old and in high school, I expect," she said to Gordie. "I'm sorry to inform you that I most certainly will not permit her to get married at this point."

"How old are you, Gordie?"

"Twenty-one, ma'am."

"Do you have a job?"

"Yes, ma'am. I'm a mechanic."

"My first husband was a mechanic," she reflected. "Not as good looking as you though. He was a fucking pig."

"I'm sorry to hear that, ma'am," countered Gordie. "But I'm not a bad person, and I would do anything in this world for Theresa."

Barbara took a drink and a lengthy pause. “Theresa, leave Gordie and me alone to see if we can reach some understanding.” Theresa did that.

“Let’s negotiate, Gordie,” Barbara said. “I have a situation you might be able to help me with. Listen carefully.

“My daughter, Caroline, Theresa and her sister Sharon’s mother, has many very serious problems. For the last fifteen years or so, she has been in one institution after another. Nothing seems to make any permanent difference.

“Last fall, she was the best she had been in years. I was so anxious to enroll Theresa in the Hillsdale-Strathroy School in Hamilton for her last year of high school that I made a bad error in judgment. I set Caroline and the girls up in an apartment in Hamilton. I even arranged for a simple job to keep Caroline occupied.

“It was a successful move from the perspective of Theresa’s schooling, but Caroline got into trouble right away. Drinking in sleazy bars, doing drugs, dragging home the biggest pieces of shit she could find. All this in front of the girls. I had to intervene, and I did.

“She’s gone back to Homewood for another dry-out/clean-up stay. And now I’m faced with what to do about the girls. I can’t let them stay alone without an adult.

“I would be willing to propose the following: you move in with the girls. It would be a good opportunity for you and Theresa to actually get to know each other, and if it works out, I might be inclined to allow you to marry when she turns seventeen.

“This arrangement would have to be very discreet. No one other than our families can know. Do you understand? I don’t want to hear from the Children’s Aid Society.”

“Yes, ma’am,” Gordie said. He was starting to feel hopeful.

“My daughter Katharine owns the building, so you will live rent-free. I pay for the utilities and my granddaughters’ schooling. I am their official guardian and am responsible for dealing with all interactions with their schools. You must never forget that the girls’ schooling comes first. Absolutely. All you would be expected to do is put food on the table.”

“That’s more than fair, ma’am.”

“Yes, it is. Your main role will be to keep my girls safe. If any harm comes to either one of them, you will face my fury, and you can’t begin to imagine it. Do you understand?”

“I do, ma’am.”

“You say that you love Theresa. This will be a real chance for you both to find out exactly how you feel. I gather by your expression that you agree to my proposition.”

“Oh, yes, ma’am, and I’m extremely grateful. I swear I won’t let you down, ma’am.”

“You’d better not. So, under the circumstances, I think you should stop calling me ‘ma’am’ and call me Barbara.”

She stood up and put out her hand. He shook it and said, “Thank you, Barbara.” Gordie knew that he had just been offered the deal of his lifetime.

“One last thing. I want to invite your parents out here so that we can meet and talk. Make that happen very soon.”

“Yes, Barbara.”

It was heavenly. Neither Gordie nor Theresa had ever known such happiness. Sharon was at the farm most of the summer, so they had the apartment to themselves. They talked endlessly about their life together and looked excitedly to the future. Theresa was pregnant.

They considered her pregnancy to be proof from a higher power that their destinies were forever intertwined. They were soul mates, and the child was their eternal bond. They believed that the baby was conceived the first time they made love.

Their bliss was somewhat tempered by the prospect of breaking the news to Barbara, so they procrastinated as long as they could.

Theresa and Gordie had spent a September Saturday afternoon at a quarry outside Hamilton with some friends. Gordie had had a few beers and asked Theresa to drive home. With his job, he didn't dare take a chance and possibly lose his license.

Theresa was an excellent driver, alert and confident. Gordie lounged in the passenger seat and watched her. He asked, "Who taught you to drive?"

"Billy," she replied. "He taught me to drive around the farm when I was fourteen, and then we went out on the back roads. He's a great driver, so I was lucky."

"Tell me about your relationship with Billy," Gordie said. "I always get the feeling he's giving me the evil eye when he's around us."

"I'm sure you're imagining it," Theresa said. "Billy has a lot on his mind right now." Gordie believed that her hands tightened on the steering wheel. "You know that he's my first cousin, and we grew up together on the farm."

"Is that all? Did you have a physical relationship?" Gordie persisted.

In their youthful naiveté, they had made a pact, right at the beginning, that they would always be completely honest with each other and truthfully answer any questions the other might ask.

"Yes, we did. Starting when I was fourteen," Theresa said.

"What was it like?"

"It was wonderful. Coming from your family, you can't imagine what it's like growing up with no hugs or kisses, no displays of affection. Sometimes Gran would pat me, and when Kathy and Eddie came to visit, they gave us many hugs and lots of love, but mainly Sharon and I would hold each other, just for human contact.

"But Billy was selfish, always disappearing, often for days at a time. I knew he was involved in things I shouldn't know about, and I was sure that included fucking lots of girls. But he did protect me and always used a condom.

"When he took me places like the beach or the drag races, he strutted around like a rooster. He acted like I was a trophy, and I hated that.

"Gran was obsessed with Sharon and I going to school in Hamilton, and Caroline was back from her latest stay in rehab. It was the best condition I'd ever seen her in, I will admit, and Gran wanted to give her the chance to be a mother to her daughters. Everybody thought it was crazy, but Gran was determined.

"I didn't believe in it, and I was really scared and begged Billy to come with us, to be our protector, but he said no. He was going to Florida to be a bartender or gigolo or drug dealer or whatever. I understood that he needed to get away from the farm, but I didn't think the Hamilton experiment would last long. And it didn't.

"Caroline headed straight to the nearest hotel, and so it began. After eight months too terrible to describe, the end came when I got a phone call late at night, telling me to come and get her right away before they called the police. She was giving blowjobs to guys in the washroom. That was just a short while before I met you.

"Gordie, please understand that there are no points of comparison between my relationship with Billy and what's between you and me."

"I'm so sorry you had to endure all that, my baby," Gordie spoke to her from his heart. He loved her so much: the most beautiful girl in the world and her little round tummy which held the child they had made.

Oh, Billy, he thought, *you stupid bastard.*

Come the beginning of October, Theresa and Gordie had no choice but to tell Barbara about the baby. They stood before her, hand in hand.

Barbara was extremely angry but had to accept that there was nothing she could do. She tore strips off Gordie, blaming him for this turn of events. Finn had never dressed him down so brutally, and he hung his head. Somewhere within him, he knew that she was right and that he should have taken care of Theresa.

Particularly distressing was the fact that the baby's arrival in the early new year was going to cost Theresa a year in her educational endeavors. As always, Gordie was sorry.

Barbara had become very fond of Gordie and unfortunately remembered every detail of her own youthful errors in judgment. She decided that there was no point in being angry and began to make plans for the wedding, scheduled for Theresa's seventeenth birthday, December 28.

Their daughter arrived in February. She was a precious bundle, with strawberry blonde hair. They named her Mary Margaret – Molly – after her grandmother.

Gordie was absolutely foolish about her. He was a doting father, helping Theresa with all the baby chores. He would change her in the middle of the night and bring her to Theresa in bed. If she fussed, he walked with her, gazing into her little face and telling her Irish stories. Theresa's heart melted with love for them both.

She and Gordie had never been closer. They believed that they were actually one person.

Theresa was taking a couple of online courses toward her diploma, and Sharon studied obsessively, getting high grades, working toward her dream of starting nursing school next year.

One night, the sisters were working at the table, and Gordie was sitting on the couch holding his baby. "Who's the best little Molly Muffin in the whole wide world?" he asked her in a teensy tiny voice.

"Honest to God, Gordie," said Sharon, "I used to think you were cool, but now you're just nauseating."

"Muffy," Gordie said confidentially, "did you know that your Auntie Sharon won a prize for being the meanest in a competition?"

"That wasn't me, you ass," Sharon retorted. "It was my cat!"

Theresa burst out laughing. "Children, children," she said. "I'm trying to work here." This back and forth went on endlessly.

A few minutes later, Sharon got up to answer the door. It was Gordie's brother Dennis. "Hello, Sharona," he said and tousled her hair as if she were a little girl.

"I swear I don't know which of you two is more annoying," Sharon said.

"It's got to be Gordie since you see him all the time," Dennis suggested.

"Well, you are more lovable," Sharon admitted. Din looked over her head at Gordie and winked.

"I've come to see the queen," he said, taking Molly from Gordie's arms.

Later, when Theresa and Gordie were in bed, she said, "What was that look Din gave you tonight?"

Gordie hummed and hawed, "I can't say."

"What do you mean you can't say?" Theresa demanded. "Gordon Finnegan, you tell me right now!"

"Well, okay," he said slowly. "But don't let on to Din and don't tell Sharon. For God's sake. You've got to promise." She promised.

"Dennis has a thing for Sharon. Has had ever since he met her. He thinks she's beautiful and smart and feisty. But he knows he's too old for her."

"That he is, some, but maybe he should focus on getting a real job while she works on her schooling. You know nothing will keep her from her goal."

Gordie pulled her close. "I'm so glad I just scooped you up immediately before you had a chance to think it over."

"I love you, Gordie," she replied.

Dennis was lovable. He was sweet-natured and affectionate. He was also extremely talented.

He was an accomplished photographer and small filmmaker. He had graduated from a media studies program a couple of years before but had found it difficult to get a job in the industry because his skills were so advanced but he had no corporate experience. He got the occasional temporary contract but couldn't land a suitable full-time job.

Meanwhile, he lived at home with his parents. Molly doted on him, and Finn tried hard not to think of him as shiftless. He picked up work tending bar or driving cab. He played bass in a neighborhood band called The Rebels which covered popular tunes and threw in a little Irish music too.

They had fun, and Gordie used to join them every now and then before the baby was born. Those were really good times because Gordie played guitar pretty well and had a great voice. The audience really warmed up when he was the front man.

Dennis had success in getting girls, but after a while, they all just wanted to be friends. His gentle ways didn't turn them on. But that was okay with him because ever since he had met Theresa's sister, he desired no other.

Sharon was so serious about her education. He figured she might beat him up if he spoke to her of romance. He was prepared to wait patiently for the right time.

The apartment was getting too small for Gordie and Theresa and their family. Molly's crib was in her parents' bedroom, and the two computer workstations and all the books and binders were in Sharon's room. It was cramped for the two girls.

Sharon was finishing Grade Twelve and had been accepted into the nursing program at the community college. Her academic record was so outstanding that she was being encouraged to go to university for a Bachelor of Science in Nursing, a four-year stint instead of two years. She wanted it, but she was anxious to make a quick start. Nonetheless, she worked every waking hour, enjoying no social life. The close quarters and the disturbance of a baby didn't make it easier.

Theresa was working online and at night school on a General Arts and Science diploma. She thought it would be a good base for whatever she decided to put her mind to later. Being a wife and mother didn't make that easier.

Gordie did well at his work. He was a first-class mechanic, and his winning personality brought customers back. His boss gave him regular raises, incentives to stay with him.

Good luck shone on the little family. An elderly widower who lived two doors down from Finn and Molly was having to leave his home. Finn had befriended him, looking after his garden and shoveling his sidewalk. The neighbor asked if Gordie and Theresa would like to rent his house. It was perfect.

They moved in early 1998. And their son, Michael-Gordon, was born in June. Such happiness! But they had to face the flip side in September when the garage where Gordie worked burned to the ground.

Gordie never expected to have difficulty getting another job, but the economy was tight, and his employment insurance wouldn't last for long. He was extremely stressed and decided to sing with The Rebels two nights a week to earn a few dollars until the situation straightened out.

As always, Gordie brought more people to the pub. Soon the band was asked to play on Thursdays as well. Word got around, and bar owners from all over town came down to listen and offer work. Soon they were working six nights a week.

The two other married guys in the group couldn't keep the pace and were replaced by local musicians. The group became "The Rebels, featuring Gordie Gallagher."

They were invited to shows featuring up and coming local talent. They were reviewed in the local entertainment paper distributed throughout the city. They appeared on the city's cable station. The crowds got bigger.

They became "Gordie Gallagher and The Rebels," and people were courting them to be their manager. Success was coming fast. It was so unexpected, and Gordie was overwhelmed. This wasn't exactly what he had in mind. It kept him away from Theresa and his kids. But he was making money, and to tell the truth, he liked the attention.

They hired a manager whose first project was to line them up with a small tour of local towns, just places around the Golden Horseshoe. Word spread. Their manager told them they couldn't lose their momentum and had to rehearse constantly. They also had to start thinking about writing some original tunes.

It was hard work, and there were growing distractions. They were exposed to increasing amounts of drugs, and women followed the band, most of them interested in getting next to Gordie.

Gordie and Dennis didn't mind blowing some dope, but they were serious about the music. The other band members were glad enough to take advantage of all the female attention, but Gordie loved Theresa. Their relationship was based on their intellectual, spiritual, and physical bond. They shared two children. He desired no one else and usually left the parties early, going to his room to call his sweetheart. They counted the days until they were together again.

Dennis dabbled in the high times, but, in his mind, no one compared to Sharon for whom he was prepared to wait as long as necessary. He wasn't a big partier, but he was making a short documentary on the rise of a local band, so he got out more than Gordie.

Gordie walked down the narrow hallway to the washroom. He felt fabulous. He had snorted cocaine a couple of times years ago when he lived down east and was camping with his cousins. Seamus, their father, would have skinned them alive if they'd been caught at home. Gordie had forgotten the amazing high.

When he came out of the bathroom, a girl was waiting in the hall, and she took his hand and pulled him through a back door into a stairwell. She pushed him against the wall and dropped to her knees. As she pleasured him, he had no thoughts other than the sensations her hungry mouth was giving him. When he came, he thought he would pass out. She stood up quickly and said, "I knew you would be delicious." And then she was gone.

He stumbled to the bathroom and splashed cold water on his face. He didn't even know who she was. In a few minutes, he went back to the party. He couldn't see her anywhere, although, in all honesty, he hadn't gotten a good look at her in the first place.

Next day, hung over from the tequila and filled with remorse, he talked to his brother about what had happened. "Do you expect me to feel sorry for you?" Dennis joked. "Seriously, man, don't blame yourself. Essentially, you were raped."

"Oh, Theresa," Gordie moaned, his face in his hands.

"Oh, my aching head," moaned Dennis.

However, it got easier to bear. The more cocaine, the less guilt.

The band spent the summer on the road, from the Victoria Day Weekend until almost Thanksgiving. They played clubs, festivals, and outdoor concerts. They were well received everywhere they went. The main draw was Gordie's good looks and charisma.

Gordie insisted that they continue to play a couple of Irish tunes each show. The band members thought he was crazy. But when he would introduce them in his Irish accent, it made the women go wild. Gordie laughed, crazy like a fox.

The band felt that they didn't need to rehearse since they were playing almost every night. They felt that they could get serious about writing once the summer was over. They felt that the excesses in which they indulged themselves were part of the job, perks after a night's hard work.

Gordie gave into the siren song of cocaine. That led to getting it on with women, many women. He was away from his wife for weeks at a time. He was twenty-five years old. He could rationalize his behavior. Dennis kept his disapproval to himself.

Sharon heard tales from her friends who followed the band. They were very bad tales indeed. She didn't say a word to Theresa, who had her own suspicions, but she did talk regularly with Din via e-mail. He sounded more and more depressed. It was apparent that he wanted to quit the band, but he couldn't bring himself to leave his brother.

Sharon was so concerned that she told Katherine everything. Kathy talked to Eddie.

Eddie was thinking about coming back east and had been for a while. The Vancouver scene was brutal, but it wouldn't be easy to get out without taking a financial beating. He suggested that Katherine return to Hamilton, find a big house which could include an office for her interior design work. Sharon could come and live there right away, and it would be a refuge for Theresa and her children when the time came. And Eddie knew it would.

Meanwhile, Katherine could do some real estate scouting work for him in the Hamilton-Toronto vicinity. He believed Hamilton would make a big comeback once the GO train came into the north-end station. He foresaw many people getting out of high-priced Toronto and moving to Hamilton once they could commute direct to Union Station.

The north end, where Finn and Molly lived, would be an up and coming neighborhood. Rundown old houses would be renovated into modern beauties, just like Finn had done years since. Eddie believed there was a fortune to be made, just around the corner.

He had total confidence in Katherine and gave her free rein. The only down side was their enforced separation.

However, they could talk or e-mail every day, and God knows, they had plenty of money to travel back and forth at least a couple of times a month.

While that prospect gave them both pause, they knew that Theresa was going to need their help soon. They didn't feel that Finn on his own could protect her. They were also a ready source of money for bail, lawyer's fees, and the like. Eddie saw serious trouble on the horizon.

January 2000

Katharine and Eddie took fish and chips to Theresa and Gordie's for dinner the evening before both Eddie and Gordie were leaving town. Gordie was very quiet, and Theresa was very tense. The presence of their two children was a good diversion.

No conversation of consequence took place, and Gordie rose from the table abruptly and said he had to get some fresh air. Eddie said he would go too. Gordie was obviously not pleased but couldn't say anything.

They went to a nearby hotel where Gordie was greeted like a celebrity. He and Eddie sat at the bar and ordered beer. After a couple of minutes, Gordie excused himself to go to the washroom, and Eddie noted a man seated at a table immediately rise and follow him. The second man was in the washroom for maybe thirty seconds before he emerged, and Gordie came out a short time later.

He looked a world better. His color was restored, and he amiably greeted other patrons on his way back to the bar. He was obviously tuned up and ordered shots of tequila for Eddie and himself.

Eddie attempted to engage him in conversation about the band and the upcoming tour, but they were interrupted by a steady stream of girls approaching Gordie. A buxom blonde told him that she just got a new car and wanted him to have a look at it. The others were less creative, but their messages were equally clear. Gordie was in his element.

Eddie recognized the futility of trying to talk to him and said he had to get going. He was flying back to Vancouver the next day, so he wished Gordie luck, put on his coat, and paid the tab. As he walked away, he heard Gordie say to the chick with the big tits, "So, Michelle, let's go and take a look at that new car of yours."

He relayed this to Katherine on the way home. She was even more upset than before and asked him what to do. "There's nothing anybody can do, Kat," he said. "He's got to hit bottom, and he's not there yet. You've got some time to talk to Theresa before he comes back, but I think that's hopeless. I believe she needs to get out now before it gets worse – and it will get much worse. And I don't think it will take too much longer.

"All you can really do is impress on her that we are ready to help her in any way, at any time. As hard as it is for us to be apart, baby, I'm glad you're here because she is going to need you."

Theresa opened her eyes in the early morning light. Her stomach churned with anxiety. Oh, God. Another day. And today Gordie was going away again. She felt a combination of relief and heartache.

He stirred and rolled on top of her, half asleep. Good. Easy. Not too wasted last night. Oh, yes. So good and easy. Sweet, sweet girl. Like home. God. And he was done.

He lifted his head and looked at her.

"T," he said, like he was surprised.

"Gordie," she whispered.

He looked into her eyes. “You’re my girl,” he said and kissed her softly.

“I love you, Gordie,” she dared to say.

“I love you too, my baby.”

The moment passed, and he said, “I gotta go,” and left her. A short time later, he was pulling out of the driveway. He didn’t wave goodbye. She wondered if she would ever see him again.

Dennis kept in touch with Sharon by e-mail. He was very unhappy and worried about his brother. He confirmed what Eddie had told Katharine about the venues they were playing ranging from seedy to scary. Drugs were everywhere, and Gordie never rehearsed, getting on stage high, and the band wasn’t any better. Supposedly, if the band was well received, they would hit the venue again on their return trip. Not too many takers were on that deal.

Eddie had told Katherine that there was only one reasonable venue, The Palladium. It was a medium-sized place, run and managed by two brothers who were interested in moving up in the live entertainment business. They ran an extremely tight ship, very serious security at the door and in the bar. The clientele was mainly college kids who had to be carefully watched for fake IDs, drugs, and weapons. The last thing the brothers wanted was to lose their license.

Dennis reported that the show at The Palladium hadn’t been too bad, unlike some of the other places where Gordie had been snorting coke backstage during the show, but the after-party at a motel next door had been reminiscent of the last days of Caligula. Din’s despair was palpable. “I can’t do it anymore, Sharon,” he wrote. “I’ve never seen such debauchery. My parents would die if they saw their son. Nothing I say makes any difference. I’m done.”

And so he was. He took a job bartending and bouncing at a local bar and worked at regaining his self-respect. Not having indulged in the low life to any great extent, he was able to return to his cheerful self fairly quickly. But he worried constantly about Gordie. In his mind, he had abandoned his brother, and he was having trouble forgiving himself

Gordie and the band staggered on. Their manager quit. Somebody's brother was supposedly filling in, but really bad went to catastrophic when they had trouble with a piece of their equipment. Not surprisingly, there was no money to address the situation, so Gordie breezily forged the old manager's name on a check for $2,500, enough to fix things and buy more cocaine.

Gordie was back at home when the police arrived to arrest him. Such a big fuss over such a small deal! Theresa, whose life had progressed from bad dream to nightmare since he had been home, was frantic. Finn, who said little, but whose stony face spoke for him, and Patrick got a family friend to represent Gordie. His bail was paid and he was released on his own recognizance until a court date was set. He was ordered to stay away from drugs and alcohol.

The children annoyed Gordie. Theresa annoyed Gordie. So the three of them spent a lot of time at Finn and Molly's. Theresa didn't say much, not wanting to betray her husband or upset his parents. She left the children there most nights and brought dinner home.

Gordie was suffering badly from withdrawal and boredom, He couldn't concentrate on anything and took his frustration out on Theresa. He fucked her constantly, most times miserably unable to finish what he started. He irrationally blamed her for everything, and her fear of him grew. Fear turned into terror when she had to tell him she was pregnant. Gordie was furious and struck her for the first time.

One night when she was lingering with Molly, afraid to go home, there was a knock on the door. Molly answered to a girl who wondered if Gordie Gallagher lived there. "He's not here right now," Molly smiled. "How can I help you?"

"My name is Darlene Seminuk, and I met Gordie in the spring. I wrote all about him in my journal, and my dad found it. He's really, really mad and going to the police because I'm only fifteen. I just wanted to give Gordie a heads up because he's such a great guy."

"Well, that's very thoughtful of you," Molly said calmly. "I'll be sure to let him know."

The girl handed her a piece of paper. "Will you give him this in case he wants to call me?" The note had a phone number written on it and, in childlike handwriting, "Remember the Palidum?"

"Excellent," Molly said enthusiastically. "You take care now."

Theresa had overheard everything and had moved from the kitchen to the front door. Back in Ireland, Molly had heard tales of the walking dead. Now she believed they were true.

"I want you to stay here from now until he goes to court," Molly said.

"I can't, Molly. He'll come for me and surely get into it with Finn. When do you suppose the police will arrive?"

They came soon enough. The additional charge of statutory rape put Gordie under house arrest with an ankle bracelet. The double charge would go before a judge in three months. Gordie was outraged. He didn't even remember the girl. What girl? There had been hundreds of girls.

His lawyer was pessimistic about the outcome. He thought Gordie might be looking at a few years in prison, and there really was no defense. Gordie paced the small house like a caged animal. He was indignant at the unfairness of it all, but he was worried nonetheless.

February 2001

The hearing was in a month's time when Gordie received a call from an old friend who had heard about Gordie's bad turn of luck. He asked if he could drop by for a short visit. When he arrived, he brought a bottle of tequila and an eight ball of coke to lift Gordie's spirits.

They shared a shot and a line, and the friend prudently said goodbye. "Now, you hide that away and make it last, Gordie. Just a little now and then to cure the blues." Gordie drank and snorted the lot during the rest of the afternoon.

The front door crashed open. "Finn, Dennis, come quick! Gordie's killing Theresa!" Sharon was in a panic. "Hurry, hurry!"

The two men tore out of the house and down the street and rushed in the door. They were completely unprepared for what they saw.

The floor and walls of the foyer were covered in blood spatters. Theresa lay, naked, on the floor, her face unrecognizable. She was lying on her side, trying to protect her unborn child, but she was bleeding profusely from her lower regions. What had gone on was apparent as Gordie, who was crouched beside her, fumbled to do up his bloody jeans.

Rage such as he had never known rushed to Finn's head. He lifted Gordie and threw him towards the stairs. Finn wanted to kill him.

"Hold him down until the police get here," Finn ordered Din. Sharon appeared in the doorway. "The police and EMS are on their way."

Finn knelt beside Theresa. He had taken off his shirt to cover her as much as he could. She was moaning softly and holding tight to his hand. He wanted to carry her to the couch, but he was afraid to move her. "Sharon," he said, "get me that blanket off the couch.

"Now go back to Molly. Get her away from the kids and tell her what has happened. Gordie's going to jail, and Theresa to the hospital. Try to soften it a bit, but she's going to know the truth soon enough," he told Sharon.

"Finn, she's my sister. I want to stay with her."

"Sharon, I will stay with Theresa now. Please talk to my wife and call Katharine. I will phone you from the hospital when you should come over.

"And, darlin', it will be okay in the end." Unexpectedly, an unusually emotional Sharon put her arms around him and said, shakily, "I love you, Finn."

Finn put his free hand out to give her a comforting pat. Both of them stared at his hand; it was dripping blood. "Finn," Theresa whispered. "Don't leave me." Sharon took off running to Molly.

The sounds of the sirens outside seemed to bring Gordie around. His brother had tied his hands to the stair railing. He was starting to struggle and spew venom at his wife and his father. His face was paper-white; his eyes were like flaming coals. He seemed to have the strength of three men, and Dennis feared he would pull the railing from the stairs.

The police arrived first and got Gordie out of the house and into the police car. One officer stayed behind. "Who are you, sir?" he asked Finn.

“I am Finnegan Gallagher, and this is my daughter-in-law, Theresa. She is thirty-three weeks pregnant.” And then he could speak no more because of the huge lump in his throat.

“Come on, sir,” one of the paramedics said kindly, helping Finn to his feet. “Let us get this young lady to the hospital.”

Theresa whispered through her broken lips, “Finn…don’t leave me…”

“You can ride with Theresa in the bus,” the paramedic said. It was hard to imagine what these people had seen and experienced. The victim was horribly injured. She had been hit in the face, breaking her nose and brutally sexually assaulted. She was bleeding profusely, but the baby’s heart was still beating.

In the ambulance, Finn sat on one side of Theresa and the paramedic on the other, monitoring.

“Finn…” It was becoming increasingly difficult to hear her.

“Yes, sweetheart?”

“Is Gordie okay?”

“He’s going to get some help, and then he can come home to us,” Although he thought he would strangle on the words, Finn somehow managed to get them out. His eyes met those of the paramedic who nodded at him ever so slightly.

When Finn got home after midnight, he was walking slowly. His face was gray. He laid his hand on Molly’s shoulder, but did not kiss her. He went directly to the liquor cabinet and poured a stiff shot of Irish whiskey which he downed.

He turned to Molly and took her hand. They sat together at the table, and at last he spoke. “The baby is alive and is being closely monitored. Theresa will be in the hospital for a while, I think. She is in awful pain.

"Sharon and Katherine came to the Emergency, and we were with Theresa when they moved her into Intensive Care. The staff said it would be best if we left now and came back tomorrow. Kathy drove me home."

Finn slowly looked around for the first time. "Where is Din?"

"He went to Patrick's to tell him what happened, and they called John, Gordie's lawyer. Gordie is in no condition to talk to anyone, but Dennis, Pat, and John went down to the police station. I'm sorry, Finn, but I can't remember anything else he said. He was crying, and Patrick insisted that he stay with them overnight."

"God knows what tomorrow will bring," Finn said. "Let's go to bed and try to at least rest a bit."

They walked silently upstairs. When they lay down, Finn kissed her tenderly and said, "I hope you can doze off, my love." And in a few minutes, exhausted and overwrought, she did.

Sometime later – five minutes? an hour? – Molly opened her eyes. Finn was sitting on the edge of the bed, his face in his hands, his body wracked with sobs. "My son. My beautiful son." Molly pulled him back down beside her and held him in her arms until dawn.

Dennis was heartsick. In his mind, he went over and over the past two years of the band. There had been so many girls, often more than one at a time.

Lying in bed one night, it came to him. He sat bolt upright. The Palladium. He had footage from that gig. It was the very last he had shot before walking away from it all. He remembered it well and the beyond-disgusting after-party. He got out of bed and rummaged through his stuff.

He found the video, and he scanned through it. Gordie was in fairly good form, and the drunken crowd loved it. In the front row was a girl dressed in an extremely short and otherwise revealing mini-dress, dancing provocatively. At the end of the last song, she whipped up her dress revealing her naked body upon which was written in green glitter: "FUCK ME, GORDIE."

Gordie threw back his head and laughed, pointing at her and calling to one of the roadies, "Bring that one to the party!"

Dennis fast-forwarded to the party. He remembered everything now and pushed on to what he was looking for. On a cot lay Gordie naked with the girl from the front row riding him. Dennis shot them straight on and then moved around and crouched behind Gordie's head. He shot the girl with her fuck-me message as he leaned in and said to Gordie, audibly on tape, "What are you doing, man? Fucking this pig and then going home to Theresa?"

"Who are you? Finn?" Gordie said contemptuously. "This has got nothing to do with Theresa." The girl was bothered.

"Go away," she said to Dennis. "Come on, Gordie. Pay attention to me!"

Dennis moved on and the tape ended abruptly soon afterward.

Next morning, he called Gordie's lawyer.

John Peterson, Gordie's lawyer, knew The Palladium as a, relatively speaking, straight arrow establishment. He knew the owners were two serious guys, and he wondered how a fifteen-year-old could have been admitted even with the snazzy new computer-generated fake IDs available. He was working on the idea that the band would have had a reasonable expectation that everyone in the crowd would be of age.

Dennis' video could be of value. The girl certainly didn't look fifteen – far from it. And she knew exactly what she wanted. Gordie was just a wasted jackass who thought everything was cool. The Palladium had already screened all the groupies.

There was no question that Gordie had had sex with a minor. It was right there on tape, but a judge just might go easier on him under the circumstances. On the other hand, a judge might be so disgusted by the tape that Gordie would have the book thrown at him.

When Gordie had completed detox at the psychiatric hospital, he was returned to the city jail. Other than meetings with his lawyer, he lay miserably on his bed. His grief and remorse were so extreme that the guards kept a close eye on him.

He would see no visitors other than Dennis. Din tried to give him little pep talks which were ignored, so he gave up. The only thing he said that made any impression was that he should at least send Theresa a note, some acknowledgment of his love and sorrow over what had happened. He said Gordie owed her something, anything other than just shutting her out.

For the first time in his life, Gordie's easy words failed him. He could say nothing or write an encyclopedia which he knew wasn't right. The last thing Theresa needed was to read a delineation of his sins. After a long time, he wrote her three lines.

The envelope was addressed in Gordie's draftsman's hand to Mrs. Gordon Gallagher. The note read:

My precious T

How can I say I'm sorry after the pain I've caused you?

How can I say I love you after everything I've done?

I pray we will meet again someday.

Gordie had decided to plead guilty to all charges in the interests of sparing his family a trial and more disgrace. His lawyer couldn't really disagree. The outcome looked very serious, but Gordie might catch a break on the rape charge. It was a small hope.

The lawyer and Gordie met with Dennis who showed them the relevant sections of the video. They amounted to less than five minutes. Gordie watched and hung his head. "My brother says our father is insisting on coming to the sentencing. I can't have him see this. I just can't do it to him."

John said, "Gordie, think it over very carefully. Making this case to the judge could shave some time, maybe a year or so, off your sentence. Don't you want to get back to your wife and family as fast as you can?"

"I don't know if my wife will ever speak to me again, and I don't want to break my father's heart. What am I supposed to do?"

"Finn is a tough guy. It will hurt him, but you know he will get past it. And if it will help you, he will take it. I can't ask the judge to look at it privately because it will have to go in the hearing transcript. The judge can suggest that Finn take a break when it is shown, but we all know how that will go."

Gordie was left to think it over. Ultimately, under pressure from John and Dennis, he agreed to the presentation of the reasonable expectation argument and the tape. He begged Din to somehow prepare their father and keep the video a secret from everyone else.

October 2001

On their way to the sentencing, Dennis said to Finn, "There will be things revealed today, Daddy, that will be very painful. Nobody comes off looking very good."

"I wouldn't expect so," said Finn stoically.

Present at the hearing were the judge, a court reporter, John, Gordie, Dennis, and Finn. Gordie's guilty plea on the fraud under $5,000 charge was accepted. He was sentenced to six months.

The Seminuks and their lawyer were present only for the statutory rape charge. Gordie pleaded guilty with extenuating circumstances. John made an effective case for reasonable expectation that everyone present at The Palladium would be over nineteen. Then the clips from the video were shown. They had to be viewed by the Seminuks and go on the record.

They were even more shocking in the sterile environment of the hearing room. Gordie sat with his hand blocking his eyes. Finn sat ramrod straight and looked directly at the screen. Darlene Seminuk's father, crimson-faced, seemed to sink into his chair. The judge maintained a neutral expression as he sentenced Gordie to time served.

Gordie's guilty plea on the domestic assault charge resulted in a sentence of five and a half years.

"Mr. Gallagher, please rise," the judge said, "I see before me another example of the evils of drugs. You will have plenty of time to think about your actions and how you have hurt yourself and others. I hope you will take advantage of the opportunities for self-improvement at the facility where you will spend the next few years. I am going to order regular psychological counselling for you in the hope that you can come to terms with yourself and make the most of your future following your release."

"Thank you, Your Honor," Gordie said as the bailiff handcuffed him. Before he was led away, he turned slightly toward Finn and said, "I'm sorry, Daddy."

"I know," replied Finn, not looking at him.

Dennis and Finn walked to the parking lot. “What do you want to do now, Daddy?” Dennis asked.

“I want to be with my wife,” Finn replied. He looked very tired, and they drove in silence.

Dennis pulled up in front of the house. “I have to go to school now,” he said.

Finn looked at him and said, “You’re a good boy, Dennis.” And he got out of the car.

After he left the band, Dennis had been accepted in the film program at York University. He had started that September and was doing exceptionally well. Almost immediately, his prodigious talent brought him to the attention of his professors and promised him a bright future.

It wasn’t easy traveling back and forth, but he had made friends and often stayed over in Toronto. At last, the fact that he was Finn’s son was apparent. He was obsessively hardworking, meticulous, and totally focused. His grades were outstanding, and he won several honors during his first year.

Not even the pain and distraction of his brother’s troubles shook his resolve. And through it all, he lived with his secret love for Sharon.

In June before Gordie’s sentencing, Sharon had graduated as a nurse at the top of her class. She had several job offers and accepted one at the Children’s Hospital. The hard work continued as she worked shifts and faced a steep learning curve. She was happy living with Katherine.

After her graduation and Gordie’s incarceration, Dennis was in the second year of his program. He wanted to move forward with Sharon. In the spirit of the last five years, he was patient, treasuring their great friendship and waiting for the right time to try to advance to something more.

He didn't see her much because of their busy schedules, but around the beginning of December, he was at Finn and Molly's when she was visiting Theresa and the children. He drove her home and gave her the present he had been carrying in the trunk of his car for a couple of months. On Kathy's veranda, he told her that he would see her at Barbara's open house on the 24th and dared to give her a loving little kiss on the lips.

Sharon was startled. Inside, she opened the gift which was wrapped in gold paper with a handmade bow. It was a framed picture taken the day of her graduation. Dennis was a superb photographer and had captured her as she was rarely seen, dressed in a yellow dress, twirling on an expanse of grass, her arms extended, a glorious smile on her face.

Tucked in the frame was a small white card with gold writing in Dennis' beautiful hand. It said: "My Sharona." Sharon looked at the picture and the card.

She was bewildered and said to Katherine, "What does it mean?"

"I'd say it means he loves you," Kathy answered.

It seemed like a long time until the open house. Plenty of time for Sharon to think things over. Finn and Molly were bringing Theresa and the baby, and Dennis was bringing Mary Francis and the other children. They traveled in tandem so that they would arrive at the same time. Finn and Dennis had agreed that someone from the family would stay with Theresa for the duration of the visit. "I'll not have those nosey old biddies from town asking her a bunch of questions," declared Finn.

Ordinarily, Theresa and the children would stay overnight at Maple Lane and join the rest of the family for Christmas dinner. This year, however, she specifically asked to stay with Finn and Molly where she felt most comfortable.

Theresa didn't want to go to the open house but went for Barbara's sake. She was a sad shadow of her former self, dressed in a plain gray dress, her beautiful hair pulled back in a bun. Her only adornment was a gold locket containing pictures of herself and Gordie. She clung to her baby.

The family rallied around her and hovered close by. It was to be a short stay.

Sharon and Dennis were only able to speak briefly away from the group. She thanked him for the special gift, and he asked when he would see her again. She was staying at the farm overnight but would come to Finn and Molly's for Theresa's birthday on December 28. "I'll see you on the 28th," Dennis said.

And then he pointed upward. "Look." They were standing in a doorway under some mistletoe.

"What can we do?" Sharon smiled, and she put her arms up around his neck and kissed him soundly.

"Merry Christmas, Sharona," he said. Right at that crucial moment, they were interrupted by Little Molly who led Uncle Din away to sing *The Christmas Song* in which he did the voices of all the Chipmunks.

"What's going on there?" asked Eddie who was standing nearby with Finn, Molly, and Katherine. "I think he's wooing her like a tiny fawn," said Katherine. The tiny fawn story had become family legend.

"But they've known each other for years," said Molly. She turned to Finn. "You were on me like a panther long, long before that."

Finn actually blushed. "Molly, my love, how much have you had to drink?" he asked amidst Katherine and Eddie's laughter. "Almost exactly enough, my love," she looked flirtatiously up at her husband.

December 28 wasn't just Theresa's birthday, it was also her and Gordie's sixth wedding anniversary. Molly was planning a subdued dinner, and no one was looking forward to attending.

Dennis arrived late but was very excited. "The documentary's all set for the polishing touches," he announced as he came through the door. "It will be ready to deliver it to the prof first thing on the second. That means he'll see it first, and we'll get his reaction soon!"

"Congratulations, son," said Finn, and his mother hugged him.

"I'm sorry for being late for your dinner, sweetie," Dennis said to Theresa and kissed her.

"Happy day to you too, Little Angel," he greeted Gabriel.

"Mommy! Where's my supper?" he demanded cheerfully. Molly bustled about, and the somber tone lightened. He patted Finn's shoulder and pulled up a chair next to him.

"I'm as hungry as a tiger, Daddy!" The children howled with laughter.

"Sing us a song, Uncle Din," one of them said.

"You know I can't eat and sing at the same time," Din sat with knife and fork in hand as Molly brought him a heaping plate.

"Why don't you kids sing a nice song for our guest of honor?"

"*Frosty the Snowman*," suggested Mary Francis, and everyone enthusiastically joined in.

Theresa smiled, and Finn and Molly looked at each other down the table. Dennis was their shining light in a very sad world.

Later, Din took Sharon home. They sat cozily in the living room, enjoying a drink while he told her some more about his project. "I'm very proud of you, Dennis," Sharon said. "I'm also proud of the way you came home tonight and cheered everyone up. It was pretty deadly before you got there.

"I'd really like to show you just exactly how impressed I am with you generally speaking. Would you care to come upstairs with me?"

"Are you trying to make this the best night of my entire life," he asked.

"I certainly hope so," and she slid over to his side of the couch. "You are a very special man," she said and gave him the most serious kiss they had shared.

Upstairs, Sharon left him in the bedroom while she went into the washroom.

Dennis was so nervous that he undressed quickly, lay down on the bed, and pulled the covers over his head.

Sharon returned to the bedroom and asked, somewhat incredulously as she got into bed, "Are you playing peek-a-boo with me?" She leaned on her elbow and pulled the bedspread down to reveal his eyes.

"No," he said in a small voice. "I'm just kind of scared."

"Scared," she asked. "Scared of what?"

"Scared of pressuring you or upsetting you or misunderstanding you," he replied. "I'm sorry, Sharona. Gordie always says I'm just a big girl."

"Well," said Sharon, "I suggest you consider where you are right now and where Mr. Know-it-all is." She pulled the covers down further and kissed him tenderly.

Dennis didn't feel scared anymore. And it really was the best night of his entire life.

January 2, 2002

Finn couldn't sleep. Not wanting to disturb Molly, he put on his robe and went downstairs. At the bottom, he heard a little sound. He turned on the lower hall light and looked into the living room.

Theresa was curled up in his easy chair, wearing his sweater, and holding her baby. She was weeping very quietly. Another knife to his loving heart.

He sat on the ottoman and said, "Sweetheart. Talk to me."

"I don't want to leave you, Finn," she eventually said. "Gordie's gone, and now I have to leave you."

Tomorrow was the day that she and the kids would be moving to Katherine's house. She had a lovely spacious apartment ready for them, and she and Sharon were excited to have Theresa there. They hoped that being away from the house where she had lived with Gordie and all the other reminders would be a positive step.

"You know that we are nearby and that you can come here any time you want for as long as you want. Think how nice it will be to be with Sharon and Kathy."

Theresa nodded tentatively.

"And you have to look at it another way: Kathy and Eddie have sacrificed a great deal for you. In spite of that, Kathy blames herself for what happened with Gordie. She talked to me about it at Christmas. She said that she was supposed to keep you from harm, but she wasn't able to do that."

"She tried to get me to leave Gordie and come to live with her," Theresa said. "But I wouldn't. She tried really hard. I thought that as long as I left the children with you and Molly most of the time he was around, I could handle him on my own."

Finn held back and said only, “That didn’t work out very well, did it?”

Theresa shook her head. She was starting to cry again.

“Please do this for me, sweetheart,” he proposed. “Give it a chance at Kathy’s. I think you owe her that. If you are unhappy, you know you can come home here. But please try, for me?”

“I’d do anything for you, Finn. You are my true father.”

“And you are my daughter. I think it’s important for all of us to try to face the future. And I would never say no if you need to come back.

“Come on now. Let me carry Gabriel, and we’ll go back upstairs.”

At her door, he gave her the baby and kissed them both. “Things will look brighter in the morning’s light, darlin’.”

Life at Katherine’s was very different. She owned a huge old house that could easily have been made into six apartments, but she had a small one-bedroom for Sharon and a big two-bedroom for Theresa. The ground floor comprised her office, a large living and dining room, suitable for entertaining, and a top-of-the-line kitchen. On the second floor was a huge master bedroom and bath for her and Eddie.

There were numerous other rooms for use as bedrooms, lounges, and storage areas.

There was a large wrap-around veranda and a three-car garage. The only thing lacking was a backyard. There was a small patio area and a garden house. Nowhere for the children to play outside.

It was winter when Theresa and the children moved in, a very cold winter, so no backyard wasn’t really a hardship although Molly and M-G had loved the deck and yard at the senior Gallaghers'. Even on the coldest day, they would spend a little time outside before coming in for hot chocolate.

Molly's new school was nearby, and she was in Grade One. M-G who was three and a half spent half-days at a day care at the same school. Theresa walked them over and back each day. Gabriel bundled up in his stroller. She enjoyed the fresh air.

Otherwise, she was lonely and bored. There was nothing to do. Katherine had a housekeeper come in three days a week and someone did the laundry twice a week. Kathy worked projects as she chose, and spent as much time in Vancouver with Eddie as his schedule would permit. Sharon was intent on learning everything about medicine and was recognized as a jewel of capability and flexibility.

She was moved from department to department, sometimes working shifts. That meant that the children had to be quiet, and it was the quiet that got to Theresa.

But the worst times were when Eddie was there or Dennis stayed with Sharon. Theresa lay awake those nights, yearning for Gordie, remembering his arms around her. She had managed to block out the bad parts and only thought of the deep love they had shared. There was no word from him, and she wondered if she would ever see him again.

In the summer, she and the children went to Maple Lane. It was better for the kids, playing outside with the dogs and cats, swimming in the pool, and getting together with their cousins, Billy's boys. For Theresa, it was actually worse. Her grandmother's unhappiness was contagious.

Emma kept quietly to herself. She was sweet and loving, but Theresa wasn't able to connect with her.

In August of the second summer at Maple Lane, Billy took her to dinner. He asked her to come to live at his house. It would be lots of fun because Kim and his sons were there a great deal of the time. Theresa and Kim went way back, and it would be good for Theresa to have a friend...besides him.

Katherine knew that the arrangement at her house wasn't making Theresa happy, and she gladly agreed to the switch. It was made before September when the children would start school. The only sad part was the distance to Finn and Molly's. Billy said not to worry about that, for Christ's sake; that's why cars were invented.

Billy's house was homey, but it could use a woman's touch. Kim didn't have time, what with her business and her own home. The boys were able to spend more time at their father's now that an adult was around during the day. They loved their cousins, Alex having a slight crush on Molly, always giving her the last cookie and pushing her on the swing. Liam found that to be kind of creepy, although he could see that Molly was pretty and really nice.

M-G thought Billy was the greatest next to Finn. He always wanted to go everywhere with him, and he liked to listen to Billy talk about the ins and outs of the landscaping business. He said, and he didn't talk much, "I want to work with you when I grow up, Billy." Billy loved the children although they had come from Gordie, whom he considered to be his arch-enemy.

Of course, Gabriel was everyone's darling, and, in an odd way, everything revolved around him.

Theresa was happy. She kept house and cooked and baked. She would walk with Gabriel in his stroller over to visit Barbara and Emma, often inviting them to dinner.

It was a real home. Although it was never discussed, Theresa wondered about Billy's relationship with Kim. They were exceptionally tight and always put up a united front for their children. Sometimes in the late evening, Billy would say that he was going to talk to Kim about some matter, and he wouldn't come home until three or four. Theresa was left to draw her own conclusions, and she wondered if Kim resented her. It didn't seem that way.

It wasn't that way. Kim loved Billy a lot, but it wasn't in a particularly romantic way. They were best friends, and he was the father of her children. She was practically twenty years older than him and had told him repeatedly that she didn't want to hold him back.

She knew that he was in love with Theresa, or at least thought he was, but she had seen enough of life to know that thwarted relationships can become obsessions over the years, no longer having anything to do with reality. She also knew that Theresa belonged to Gordie. Nobody knew what Gordie would be like when he was released from prison, and Kim hoped that Theresa's love for him wouldn't become one of those obsessions.

In 2003, after Barbara's Christmas Open House, Billy and Theresa were wrapping presents and placing them under the tree. Alex and Liam were at home with Kim, the others asleep upstairs. Five hyper children on Christmas Eve was too much to ask of anyone.

When they were finished, Billy lit the tree lights and said, "How's about a shot of Bushmill's?" Theresa wasn't much of a drinker; she had spent too much time being pregnant and nursing.

"Should I?" she asked hesitantly.

"Certainly. You've got to honor your Irish heritage," he said, pouring two shots.

"My Irish heritage," she laughed, "I don't have an Irish bone in my body!"

"Not anymore," said Billy who had already had a few drinks.

"Billy, you're awful," Theresa blushed, but she giggled and drank the shot. He quickly filled her glass again, and they toasted once more. They set down their glasses.

"I love you, Teri," he said, taking her by her shoulders and kissing her with his heart on his lips. Her head was spinning, and she clung to him. No one had loved her for so long.

Afterward, she cried and cried. Billy was dismayed. "I'm sorry, darlin'," he said. "I should never have done that."

"It was my fault too, Billy," she sobbed. "Do you want me to leave your house?"

That was the last thing Billy wanted. He hadn't given up hope. "Of course not," he said. "Let's just put this in the file folder with everything before 1995, okay?"

And it was okay. The incident just seemed to go up in a puff of smoke, and life continued on in the same pleasant vein. In 2004, Molly was eight years old, M-G was six, and Gabriel was a lovable and precocious three, "almost four" as he liked to describe it.

Billy's landscaping business continued to grow, and Kim became more and more successful. She hired more staff and cut back on her own schedule. She wanted to enjoy her children before they went away to school. The time passed by so quickly.

But it was not so quickly for Theresa who lived for the day she would see Gordie again. She knew that Dennis was in regular touch with him, but she refused to put him on the spot by asking questions. Gordie would come for her when he came for her.

Whenever the family all got together, Billy would be sulky and ill-tempered afterwards. Being around the Gallaghers and seeing how Theresa was one of them invariably put him into a jealous snit. After Gabriel and Molly's joint birthday party at Barbara's in February 2005, where he had had too much to drink, he came home to further indulge himself.

The children were in bed, and he was sitting at the table. Theresa passed by and stopped to straighten the place mats. "Why are you still wearing that?" he demanded, meaning her wedding ring.

"Because I'm married," she replied.

"Married to the guy who beat the fuck out of you and almost killed Gabriel. You're supposed to be my wife, Theresa Campbell," he slammed down his glass and stood up.

Theresa was frightened and moved toward the phone. He grabbed her wrist. "Don't," he said. "Don't." They stood looking at each other for a long minute. He loosened his grip. "You know I could never hurt you," and he raised her hand to his lips and kissed it.

He turned and left the house, and she heard him drive away.

She was very alarmed by what had happened. She didn't feel that she had the strength to deal with any more. She believed that she would have to take the children and go back to Kathy's.

The long night passed, and Billy didn't come home. Theresa assumed he had gone to Kim's, and she would deal with him the next day. She decided during the sleepless hours that she would try to work things out with him because she didn't want anyone to know what had happened between them.

In the morning, however, he did not return. She didn't want to call Kim's, so she waited and worried.

Billy had indeed spent the night at Kim's. She had managed to get him to stop drinking and calm down. Over coffee the next day, he said he had to go and talk to Dennis. He had to find out when Gordie was expected to be released.

He drove into Hamilton and found Dennis sweeping the light overnight snowfall from his parents' sidewalk and deck. They sat together in Billy's truck, and Billy came straight to the point.

"It's not right for me to ask you this," he told Din, "but I have to know when Gordie will be coming back. Do you know? Will you tell me?"

Dennis did know but had promised that he would not share that information with anyone. However, Billy was obviously very upset. Din knew that he was in love with Theresa and recognized that the wait for Gordie's unspecified return must be hell. It touched his well-known soft heart, something that Billy had hoped for.

"All I know," Dennis said slowly, "is that Gordie has done very well and will not be detained the full six years. He will be released sometime this year, maybe summer or fall."

Summer or fall. Billy put his head down on the steering wheel.

"I'm sorry, Billy. But it is better that you know it's coming rather than just have him show up at your door one day."

"Has he said he wants Theresa back?" Billy asked.

"He doesn't talk about her at all," Dennis replied truthfully. "I think the subject is too painful for him. But I know how much he loved her before he got messed up, so I would definitely think so."

"Din, you're a friend, and I thank you," Billy shook his hand. "I really must be getting back now."

Billy drove to Dunnville on autopilot. In no time at all, Theresa would be gone. Forever.

When he got home, he said to Theresa, who was very anxious, "I'm sorry, Teri. It won't happen again," and he went into his office and closed the door.

A black cloud hung over the house for the next several weeks. Billy didn't talk at all. He stayed in his office or in his bedroom with the door shut. He did come to the table for supper, but the atmosphere was so dark that it affected the children.

Sensitive Molly would burst into tears for no obvious reason. Gabriel reverted to being a four-year-old and always wanted to sit on his mother's lap. A few times, Theresa saw Alex and Liam holding hands. It was hard to know what M-G was thinking; he had always been taciturn.

Most nights, Kim came to dinner too to support Theresa. Other than picking up the boys or dropping them off, Billy didn't visit her.

At the end of March, it was the children's March Break. Theresa bundled everyone up and went to Katherine's. Kim took Alex and Liam to Victoria where she had friends. Billy was alone.

When they returned, he had painted the interior of the house. He must have worked day and night, and it looked great. He had placed flowers in the dining room, living room, and Theresa and Molly's bedroom. When he and Theresa were alone, he said only, "Let's move forward." She agreed, and the tension lifted.

April was the start of Billy's busy season, and that helped tremendously. However, Theresa never completely relaxed. Life was not the same.

June 2005

Theresa kissed her children and, after some motherly fussing, waved goodbye as the van pulled out of the driveway. Billy and Kim were so good to take the kids for a day at a water park in celebration of M-G's birthday. And it was nice to have a day to herself.

She did a load of laundry and hung it out to dry. As she pinned up the last sheet, she felt a presence behind her. She turned and saw Gordie approaching. She flew over the grass into his arms.

He was shaking, and she could feel his heart pounding. "Forgive me. Please forgive me," he whispered. "Please say you'll take me back."

"I never let you go," she said.

Later, Gordie told her that he had been in touch with his cousin Seamus O'Connor in Nova Scotia. Gordie had lived with the O'Connor family for five years before he met Theresa when he returned to Hamilton in 1995.

Seamus owned a service center and had offered Gordie a job as a mechanic. Gordie was going there to make a new start and wanted Theresa to come with him. She said that she would never be without him again and agreed to leave the next day.

The hard part was what to do about the children. The really hard part was going to be her confrontation with Billy that evening. Gordie wanted to stand with her when that happened, but she said that she had to face him alone. Gordie would stay in a motel nearby and come to the house in the morning.

Having to say goodbye until tomorrow was agonizing. But they both were strengthened by the knowledge that the rest of their life together stretched before them.

When Billy and Kim got home with the kids, it was around 6:30. He looked at Theresa standing on the porch as he was unloading the van, and he knew. Kim was herding the overtired group into the house, telling Alex and Liam that they would be going home in a few minutes while the others hugged Theresa and ran inside for juice.

Billy came last, carrying a couple of bags of towels and damp bathing suits. "Good evening, Mrs. Gallagher," he said, "Where would you like these?"

"How was your day?" Theresa asked nervously.

"Not as good as yours, I'm sure," he replied.

"Shall I put them out back?"

"Please," she said.

"When will you be leaving?" he asked.

"Can we please talk about this later?" she said quietly.

"Whatever you say, ma'am. At your service, ma'am."

Kim appeared in the doorway. She had overheard their exchange. "What do you want me to do?" she put her arm around Theresa.

"Come here tomorrow morning at ten o'clock."

"Where is he?"

"At Gulliver's Inn."

"When are you leaving?"

"Tomorrow, but I have to ask Billy if the kids can stay."

"I will help you any way I can. And he loves the kids."

"I know."

"Stop talking before he comes back. I'll be here tomorrow at ten."

She called to her sons and hugged Theresa. "I can be here in five minutes if you need me."

The children were in bed early. They were exhausted after their wonderful day. Theresa felt like throwing up.

She and Billy faced off in the kitchen. Many things were said, bitter, stinging things, things that might be forgiven in time but would never be forgotten.

In response to Billy's rant against her and Gordie, she clarified once and for all that Gordie had not "stolen" her; Billy had lost her through his careless arrogance and selfishness.

"At the time when I needed you most, when Sharon and I needed you most, when we had to go and live with Caroline, you went off for a road trip adventure with your pig friend, Randy. You have no idea what we went through. We were fifteen and sixteen years old." That slowed Billy down. He could not deny the charge.

"And you slag Gordie for what happened. You'll do well to remember that you were doing drugs and dealing when you were sixteen, running with that wild crowd in Hamilton, and fucking every slut you could stick it in. And so much more. If you hadn't gotten involved with Kim, you could have ended up just like Gordie, so spare me your self-righteousness."

"But I loved you," he countered.

"Did you?" she asked. "All I ever heard was 'you're mine' and 'you belong to me.' Gordie didn't treat me like a possession. He treated me like I was beautiful and special."

"In addition to him being so tall and handsome and such a great lay?"

Ultimately, after the angry words, when it was perfectly clear that she was leaving with Gordie tomorrow one way or another, Billy agreed to keep the children. He couldn't bear losing them too.

August 2005

A warm summer evening in Antigonish, Nova Scotia and Gordie and Theresa relaxed in the afterglow with gentle kisses and murmured words meant for no one but each other.

Theresa couldn't contain her excitement any longer and announced that a tiny person they had made was growing inside her. Gordie flushed deeply and began to cry. He buried his face in the special place between her neck and her shoulder. "Jesus Christ," he sniffled, "I've turned into a girl since I got out of jail."

Theresa brushed the hair from his eyes and said soothingly, "You and I both know that isn't true. It's just that the walls you had to build around your heart are breaking down."

"Theresa Katherine," he said, "you are my angel of redemption. I will love you until my last breath and beyond." She purred contentedly in his arms.

November 2005

Theresa was five-months pregnant and so radiant in her happiness that people on the street would take a second look.

She and Geordie loved living in Antigonish. His mother's cousins, the O'Connors, were generous, open-hearted people. They had been helpful in every way and included the Gallaghers in all their family celebrations for which no real reason was required. The fun of being together was reason enough.

Their house required a fair amount of renovating, and everyone pitched in. They donated furniture and domestic accessories to help until Gordie could afford to buy what they needed.

Theresa wrote letters and postcards to the children every week. She made up little games which they played by mail. Every second Sunday, she and Gordie had lengthy phone calls, talking to each child and hearing all the news. The children were in good spirits and were always waiting by the phone for their parents' call. Theresa and Gordie were hopeful that they would want to come to visit in the coming summer months after their new baby was born.

Everything was going well, and as their child's arrival grew closer, Theresa and Gordie decided to come home for a brief visit at Christmas. Gordie dreaded facing everyone, but he wasn't about to let Theresa go alone. He had sworn to himself that he would never leave her alone for longer than a working day. His love for her and his gratitude for his second chance grew steadily stronger. She was his cherished darling.

Christmas 2005

Din and Sharon picked them up at the airport on their way to the farm. Sharon threw her arms around Gordie and said, "I'm so glad you're back!" Gordie felt his emotions well up; he hadn't known what kind of reception to expect from her. He had found it hard to imagine that she could ever forgive him.

Sharon had been there for the cocaine psychosis nightmare. In the meantime, however, she had become a nurse, and she understood a great deal more about drugs and their effects on users. She understood the difficult concept that the insane monster who had attacked Theresa wasn't really Gordie.

Her heart had ached for them both. Theresa was a devastated woman and Gordie a broken man as Dennis described him after his early prison visits. He remembered only flashes of that terrible night, and in spite of his regular court-ordered psychiatrist appointments, he could find no peace or self-forgiveness.

Time passed, and Gordie gained more understanding of what had brought him to this place. He wanted to live a good life and be with his wife and children. He took courses and upgraded his professional skills. He attended meetings for prisoners with substance-abuse problems. He helped other prisoners learn to read.

He did so well that he was assigned to work in the prison garage. Gordie was an excellent mechanic and had a good attitude, and his supervisors were impressed. With mixed feelings, they talked to administration about his being considered for early release.

As a model inmate, Gordie was allowed to use the computers in the library, and he started to communicate with his cousin Seamus in Nova Scotia. Seamus was aware of Gordie's fall from grace, but he knew him as a good person and a natural mechanic.

Seamus offered Gordie a job at his service center when he was released if he were allowed to leave Ontario.

After three years' incarceration, Gordie was directed to meet with a counsellor to talk about the possibility of early release. Because of his exemplary behavior, efforts at self-improvement, and contributions to the institution and other prisoners, he was a serious candidate for parole.

Seamus wrote a letter explaining his relationship with Gordie since he was a boy of sixteen and his desire to help Gordie and himself by hiring him and acting as his sponsor.

It took months, but ultimately the decision was made that Gordie would be released in June of 2005. At that point, he would have served three years and eight months of his six-year sentence. He would report to a parole office in Hamilton immediately after his release and to another in a town not far from Antigonish when he arrived in Nova Scotia.

Gordie would be released in a couple of months, but he asked Din to keep that information secret. He also asked Din to get him a vehicle which would make it to Nova Scotia after he went to Dunnville to see Theresa.

Dennis had shared all this with Sharon, and her optimistic spirit believed in a happier future. She knew that Theresa would never choose to stay with Billy and turn Gordie away. She knew that Theresa, while grateful to Billy, belonged to Gordie heart and soul.

And that's how it had played out. In the interests of not uprooting their children when they didn't have a definite plan for a home in Antigonish, Theresa begged Billy to keep the children while she and Gordie went ahead and got organized.

Billy, in spite of his extreme anger and bitterness toward them both – "Certainly I'll look after your kids while you and Gordie enjoy your honeymoon." – loved the children as if they were his own. He agreed to keep them. The three adults managed to agree to defer to whatever the children wanted to do. To everyone's relief, they wanted to stay in what was really the only home they had ever known.

The children would be at the farm for Christmas, and Finn and Molly were coming too. Gordie's stomach churned at the prospect of seeing Finn, but there would be a lot of people there, and Theresa had promised not to leave his side.

Dressed up in its seasonal finery, the magnificent old house looked like a Christmas card. The big family was gathered, and laughter and scraps of conversation mingled with the quiet background music. *Barbara always throws a beautiful party*, thought Finn as he followed his hostess to the atrium to look at the rust on her Boston ferns. Suddenly, he felt a small hand slip into his.

He looked down at the sweet face of his most beloved grandchild, Gabriel, the child Theresa had almost lost. He was a tiny boy. He was bright, perceptive, loving, and possessed the same otherworldly qualities as his aunt, the universally adored Mary Frances. His verbal skills were remarkable, and people loved to talk to him to get his take on things.

Gabriel was four and ten months old, but, the day after each birthday, he always pronounced himself to be "almost…"

This was very important to him, for some reason, and respected by everyone. At the moment, he really was "almost five."

"Gampa," he said, "come," and pulled him into the great room through the crowd straight to Gordie and Theresa. Gabriel stopped and put Finn's hand in Gordie's hand.

"There," Gabriel said with satisfaction. "Twins." Finn and Gordie looked at each other, neither having the faintest idea what to say or do. Finally, "Merry Christmas, son. You look well." And in that strange way, the slow healing process began.

Later, Theresa told Molly that the morning she and Gordie left Billy's house to go to Antingonish, they talked to the children to explain what was happening and how everything might be handled.

The children were sitting at the dining room table when Theresa brought their father into the room. Immediately, Gabriel slid off his chair, went straight to Gordie, and attached himself to his leg. He had never seen Gordie before. Theresa speculated that it was because Gordie looked so much like Finn whom Gabriel adored.

In the presence of both men, Gabriel was happy and content, moving from one to the other, kisses for both.

Four days later, on December 28, many members of both families gathered again at Barbara's. It was the celebration of Theresa's 27th birthday and Gordie and Theresa's tenth anniversary.

Billy refused to attend and was sitting at the dining room table with a bottle of Jack Daniels when Kim brought the boys home. The other three kids were staying with their parents at Maple Lane.

"How was the party?" he asked Alex and Liam.

"It was great," said Alex enthusiastically.

"Everybody was crying," elaborated Liam. "You should have seen it, Daddy."

"Everybody was crying?"

"Yep. Din gave Sharon a big ring!"

It had become a tradition for Dennis to propose to Sharon during the Christmas season, in front of everyone, only to be told that she loved him but he wasn't mature enough to get married. Dennis always took it in good spirits, saying that he would try harder for next year.

"By God, she said yes," and Billy looked at Kim for details.

"He has a 'real' job starting January 2 with the CBC in Hamilton," said Kim. "Everyone was really happy for him. Molly started to cry at that point.

"Then he said, 'Sharon will you please, please marry me now?' Sharon looked astonished, and then she said, 'Yes, I will.' Everybody hooted and hollered and started crying. Dennis too.

"He reached into his pocket and pulled out a diamond ring and dropped to one knee. He put it on her finger, and she asked him if he'd been carrying it around all these years. He said no, he couldn't afford it until now.

"It was pandemonium. I've never seen Barbara so happy, and Finn looked better than he has in years. It was truly wonderful."

"That's real nice," said Billy. "They're a great couple. She makes him tougher, and he makes her softer."

"Gordie gave Theresa a ring too, Daddy," Liam innocently informed his father. "He made a speech and gave her a ring with writing in it."

"What did it say?" Billy asked.

"I can't remember, but everybody was really crying then," Alex answered.

"Come on, weirdo," he said to his brother. "Let's go play with our new stuff," and they jostled each other up the stairs.

"Would you care to tell me about that, Kimberly?" Billy looked at Kim. She had been dreading this part, but somebody was going to tell him, so it was better that she did it in the privacy of his own home.

"Well, Gordie toasted Theresa for her birthday and said that it's impossible to describe how happy he is to be here with her for their tenth anniversary.

"He said that when they got married, in his 'youthful arrogance' he called it, he had given her a ring with his name engraved in it."

"That's true," Billy said, pouring himself a shot of Jack.

"This time, he was giving her a new ring with a more appropriate inscription," Kim paused. She didn't want to continue.

"Tell me."

"It says, 'Two Hearts… One Soul.'"

Billy's face turned beet-red. "And everybody cried," he said and tossed back the shot.

He pushed his chair away from the table, picked up the bottle, and walked out the back door.

Early next morning, Gordie was wakened by a light kiss on his forehead. He groggily opened his eyes to see Gabriel standing by the bed. "What's going on, buddy?" he asked quietly, putting his arm out to embrace his little son.

"I want to come to stay with you and Mommy," Gabriel whispered.

"I want that too," said Gordie, "but you know we're going to have to talk about it."

"Yes."

"Come on and get in bed, and we'll let Mommy sleep a little more, okay?" He lifted the covers, and Gabriel cuddled up in his arms. In just the short time Gordie had spent with the child over the holidays, he had come to love him second only to Theresa. He was just a little boy, not quite five years old, but he seemed so grown up a great deal of the time.

"Today we'll talk to everybody and work it out," Gordie whispered.

Billy had a hangover and was in a very bad mood. Kim had called after breakfast, asking him to bring the boys to Maple Lane for lunch. He didn't understand why she couldn't have picked them up on her way there.

However, he agreed, put on his sunglasses, and drove Alex and Liam over. He gave them each a loony to be really quiet in the car. He pulled into the parking area and let them out. Barbara appeared on the veranda and beckoned him to come along.

What now? he thought. *I'm not staying for lunch.*

Barbara took his arm and kissed him. Alex and Liam had already run inside. "Billy, I want you to come in the house. It's important, and I want you to do it for me."

"Only for a minute," he stipulated, feeling too poorly to argue.

In the great room, a fire was burning, and Kim and all the kids were sitting around on the couches and easy chairs. And Gordie, tall, good-looking motherfucker. And Theresa, pregnant and more beautiful than he had ever seen her. *Oh, God, why am I here?* he silently asked.

He took off his sunglasses and sat on the arm of his grandmother's chair.

Discussion had obviously already been taking place, and his input was required. Gabriel wanted to go to Antigonish with Gordie and Theresa for a visit of a length to be determined by Gabriel as he went along. Everyone was being very positive and flexible, except M-G who said straight out, "I don't want him to go."

Maybe the visit would be for a week, two weeks, a month, whatever Gabriel wanted. He was adamant, however, that he had to be back home in time to go to kindergarten in the fall.

Billy had a feeling in his chest like thin ice cracking underfoot. He loved Gabriel on a level with his own children. Gabriel ran across the room to him and put up his arms. Billy lifted him and buried his face in his little shoulder.

"I love you, Billy," Gabriel said.

"I'm coming back."

"Well then, you'd better have a great time while you're there," Billy replied in a voice that didn't sound quite right.

He set Gabriel down and said, "I'll be back in a few minutes," and walked out to the veranda.

On New Year's Eve, Gordie sat on Gabriel's bed. They had lived through three action-packed days, and now they were home in Antigonish, happy and tired. Theresa had kissed her baby goodnight and gone to lie down for a little while.

Gabriel held his father's hand. "I'm glad I'm here, Daddy."

"You can't know how happy your mommy and I are to have you, buddy," Gordie replied.

"I do know," said the little boy.

"If you get lonesome in the night, you come next door and climb in bed with us, okay?"

"I will," Gabriel said sleepily. Gordie kissed him and tucked him in. As he left the bedroom, he felt a wonderful warmth course through his body. This time last year, he had been in prison.

Late every morning, Theresa walked carrying a little cooler to the service center where Gordie worked. She did this for three reasons: she was pregnant and needed some exercise and fresh air; she liked to take Gordie a fresh hot or cold lunch, depending on the season; and she wanted to be with Gordie, even for just a few minutes.

Gordie's workmates teased him, calling him spoiled and Theresa's wee boy. They weren't laughing, however, when they saw his wife's beautiful smile and watched him eat his special lunch while they had mundane sandwiches and pudding cups.

Now Theresa had a companion. She called Gabriel her "Happy Hopper" because he never walked. He hopped and skipped and tried to catch squirrels to be his friends. He had endless questions about the houses, the trees, the birds, and the occasional dog or cat that would happen by.

The shopkeepers came to know him. His friendliness and boundless curiosity about everything made him a favorite. Everybody would take time to talk with him while his mother shopped. He became known as "Gordie and Theresa Gallagher's adorable little son."

Back home, Gabriel had a bunch of grown-up cousins and a couple of little baby ones. That was nice, but in Antigonish, he had lots of cousins of all ages. And they were really fun!

Billy used to freeze a rink in the yard if the weather was cold enough so Gabriel and his sister and brothers all learned to skate. He had started out with baby skates with two blades, but since he was "almost four," he had skates like his brothers.

They hadn't been packed in the last-minute rush, so his cousin Robby O'Connor gave him his old ones. Robby was growing like a weed, his mother said, so the skates were in fine condition.

Almost every weekend there was a skating party. If it wasn't too cold, there would be a fire and everybody would toast marshmallows and drink hot chocolate from thermoses. The O'Connors were always singing and laughing, so these were great times.

In February, it was Gabriel's birthday and he was "almost six." He got so many presents; it took ages to open them. And his mommy made a huge birthday cake with two layers: one was chocolate and the other was yellow. There were Smarties all over it!

Gran sent him a disposable camera to take pictures of the party and an album to put them in. The very first picture was of Gabriel on the ice, looking sharp and proud in the candy cane-striped scarf, hat, and mitts that Gamma Molly had knitted for him. The second picture was of him with the toboggan he got from Mommy and Daddy.

That album was filled with happy pictures in no time flat. Gabriel thought Antigonish was a great place, and the weeks flew by.

At the beginning of April, his mommy had a new baby. She and Daddy asked him what he would suggest for a name. Kitten Flower sounded nice to him, and everybody else thought so too. They all laughed and hugged him.

Mommy and Daddy explained that they were going to call her "Joy" because that is what she had brought them. Barbara would be her first name, and Kitten Flower her third. Daddy said it was really special to have three names, like the princes and princesses in England. Wow!

To our dear family and friends

Gordie and I are thrilled to announce the arrival of our daughter, Barbara Joy Kitten Flower Gallagher, on April 8, 2006.

Weighing six pounds, she fit easily into her father's waiting hands. She is a sleepy little girl, only making tiny mewing sounds when she requires attention. We sit and watch her endlessly, marveling at the miracles that brought her to us.

Her formal name is splendid: Barbara (for her great Gran, Barbara Campbell) Joy Kitten Flower (chosen by her big brother Gabriel who is "almost six"). We have decided to call her Joy on a day-to-day basis because she symbolizes our overwhelming happiness and gratitude and the eternal love we share.

With every best wish to you all,

Theresa and Gordie

Billy sat in front of the computer in his office. He had a glass of Irish whiskey in hand and was prepared to feel very sorry for himself. He finally opened the e-mail from Theresa entitled "Joyous News!"

He read it over and over. He looked at the attached photographs: a tiny naked rosebud with a mop of black hair cradled in Gordie's hands, the same little flower dressed in pink with a small pink bow in her unruly mane. She was not his child. She was Gordie's. Theresa was not his wife. She was Gordie's. The message was absolutely unequivocal: "the eternal love we share."

Billy reached for the bottle to pour himself another shot. Suddenly, a voice spoke to him. It came from inside his head, but it sounded suspiciously like Kim.

"So, Billy," the voice said, "why not have another drink? You could be passed out by dinnertime instead of enjoying your children on this gorgeous Sunday afternoon.

"Aren't you ready to admit that you are all alone in your misery? Are Theresa and Gordie unhappy? Are they brooding about you?

"The hands are racing around the clock. The days of you and Theresa ended in 1994. Look around you: you have five wonderful children who love you, a successful business, a nice home, and someone who will stand beside you through thick and thin. Dig it, my friend. It's time to live your life."

The voice was so strong that he swiveled in his chair to see if Kim really was in the room. She wasn't, but he got up and put the bottle away. It was indeed time.

He turned off the computer and walked out into the sunshine. He watered his dogs and drove to Kim's.

"My love, come and see the e-mail Theresa sent us. There are pictures of our new granddaughter," called Finn.

Molly hurried into the room and scooted a chair over beside him at the computer. Together they laughed over "Kitten Flower."

"That blessed little boy," said Molly.

The pictures were wondrous, and Molly said, "That looks just like Gordie in your hands after he was born. So incredibly beautiful!"

"He was a good deal more vocal as I recall," said Finn.

"Oh, Finn, let's go down to see them, just for a weekend," Molly implored.

"They'll be here in September for Dennis and Sharon's wedding, my love," he replied.

"I can't wait that long, Finn. Please, please."

"You can play me like an instrument, my tiny fawn," he sighed.

Molly giggled. "Let's check with Theresa to see what's convenient for them."

Molly hopped up and started rummaging through the trunk that held all her craft materials. "I'm going to crochet a little outfit for Joy. Bright pink to suit her coloring, not that washed-out pastel."

For a long while, Finn stared at the picture of the child in her father's hands. He felt the stab of the pain that never really went away. "My son," he whispered so softly that Molly was able to pretend she hadn't heard.

Wool in hand, she came up behind him. "I love you, Finnegan," she said and placed a kiss on top of his head.

Finn and Molly came to meet Joy the first week in May. They had only come for a long weekend.

It was a busy visit with the O'Connors hosting a big party for them on Saturday night. Molly spent a lot of time fussing over the baby, and she baked all Saturday morning. She made goodies for the party and many treats for Theresa's freezer. They would go in Gordie's special lunches. Everybody was happy.

Gordie took his father to see the service center and introduced him around the town. Finn was pleased to see how well people responded to his son, and Seamus told him privately at the party that Gordie was his number one mechanic, superior to his own son Brendan because of his exceptional interpersonal skills. Seamus said that customers would book appointments for their vehicles and specifically ask for Gordie.

It would appear that the boy had turned his life around.

With Gordie and Theresa's permission, Molly asked Gabriel if he would like to fly home with them. He said no, he wasn't ready to leave his parents and baby sister. His grandmother and grandfather were a little disappointed, but it was certain that he would be back for school and Sharon and Dennis' wedding on Labor Day Weekend.

Although Barbara had bought Gordie a computer for his birthday in March before Joy was born, Theresa and Kim liked to talk on the phone on a regular basis. They had known each other for a long time and were good friends. They were able to be perfectly frank with each other.

Kim told her that Billy was very disappointed that Gabriel hadn't chosen to return with Molly and Finn after their May visit. Theresa suggested that they come with all the children for a visit in July, and she would bet that Gabriel would come back with them.

Gordie had booked a cottage on Prince Edward Island for a week, and Theresa thought it would be a good time for the kids, a week in Antigonish and a stay on the Island. She was anxious that Molly and M-G visit Nova Scotia and meet their new sister. She hoped that they would be comfortable there and want to come often.

Kim agreed that it was a good idea, but Billy couldn't come too, not because of his attitude, but because it was his busy season. She said that his business was booming, and he had hired a couple of students from the Landscaping Program at a local community college to work with him for the summer.

She said that she was very proud of him and that he seemed happier than he had been in a long time, although he pined for Gabriel. She said he now referred to Gordie by name and didn't call him "that goddamn bastard" or the like. The change seemed to have come around the time of Joy's birth. Thank God!

Anyway, they would all meet at Sharon and Dennis' wedding in September. Billy had actually said of course he would go.

There was great excitement in Ontario and Nova Scotia as everyone got ready for the July adventure. Kim and the children would fly to Halifax where she would pick up a rental van. Gordie and Theresa could travel in their car with their baby, and Kim would chauffeur the kids.

Everything about the two-week holiday was perfect. Kim and company did some local touring, and the five children loved it. They camped in the backyard some nights, swam and fished, enjoyed picnics and barbeques with the O'Connors, and Little Molly and M-G spent time with their parents and Joy.

One morning on P.E.I., Gordie and Gabriel were up early and went for a walk on the beach. After many questions about everything, Gabriel asked Gordie, "Do you know that I'm going to go back with Kim and the kids?"

"I know it's time, but it's really hard to see you go," replied his father.

"They need me, Daddy, and I'll see you at the wedding," the little boy said, tightening his hold on Gordie's hand.

"Can I come back next year?"

"You can come back any time you want," said Gordie. "This is your home too you know,"

"I know," said Gabriel, but he looked a little sad.

Gordie crouched down and said, "I'm going to tell you a big secret that you can carry in your heart until we see you in September. Mommy's going to have another baby next spring. So maybe you can come down around Easter with Gamma and Gampa for a little visit before you come in the summer. What do you think about that?"

"Did you make a boy this time?"

"I don't know, son. It's always a surprise. It could be a puppy."

Gabriel laughed and said, "That's silly!"

He put his arms around his father's neck and hugged him tight. "You're my very own daddy," he declared.

Labor Day Weekend 2006:

There had been a family pool as to when this day might come. Patrick's wife, Linda, was the lucky winner. Everyone was happy, although some said they'd believe it when they saw it.

The wedding at Barbara's home was to be exactly to Sharon's specifications. No extravagance, no fussiness or "la-di-da" as she described it. It was a simple civil ceremony before Barbara's lawyer, Theresa, and Gordie in attendance. There were no dress-up for the wedding party or guests, and no bouquets or boutonnieres. She just wanted a great party which everyone would always remember.

In the last few minutes before the boys would arrive to walk them downstairs, Sharon and Theresa talked. Sharon was pacing, and Theresa asked her if she was nervous. “Wouldn’t you be nervous if you were about to marry a giant toddler?” she snapped.

“I thought he was doing a lot better since he got a real job,” Theresa said mildly.

“Well,” Sharon replied, “I do have to admit that. But I never know when he will get a hare-brained idea and move us to some godforsaken place so he can make a sad documentary while I try to help people with no medical facilities, supplies, or probably even running water. I have to be constantly vigilant against his big heart and generous ways.”

Theresa bit her lip to keep from laughing. “I’m sure you can keep him under control,” she said.

“You’ve been together a long time. You love him dearly?” she asked rhetorically.

Sharon’s eyes filled with tears. “I do. But don’t you ever dare tell anyone. And I don’t need any sentimental slop right now.”

The pair hugged just as Gordie called through the door that it was time.

The brothers looked handsome and, although Dennis feared he would get into deep trouble, he gave Sharon a long-stemmed pink rose to carry. Her face got all soft, and she said, “Oh, Dennis. You just can’t follow instructions.”

Gordie and Theresa looked at each other and tried to remain straight-faced.

They descended the beautiful old staircase and approached a small table which was covered in one of Barbara’s lace cloths. There were no flowers.

In less than five minutes, everything was done, including the signatures on the marriage certificate. Gordie spoke to the guests: "Everyone, it is my extreme pleasure to introduce our little sister and my brother and best friend, one of the most mature guys I know, now and forever to be known as 'Dennis and Sharon Gallagher.'

"God, I hope I got that right," Gordie looked at Sharon. She nodded approvingly and, unexpectedly, threw her arms around Dennis and kissed him passionately. He turned his head toward the cheering, applauding group and with a smile of pure sunshine said, "She loves me."

Oh, what a wonderful party!

Billy's irrepressible sons, Alex and Liam, were bouncing on the spot. "Daddy, Daddy, there's a whole pig cooking in the yard, and salads all over the place. And stuff we don't know what it is."

"Then we'd better get some drinks and go out and have a look," said Billy.

"Perhaps a double scotch for you, my sweetness," he asked Kim, laughing.

"I think you're right," she told him.

The buffet was amazing, and the venue was gorgeous. The guests enjoyed the beautiful late afternoon at tables with umbrellas on the lawn and patio. The exuberant children were corralled on the big verandah. Dennis had put together some discs he called "The Greatest Tunes of All Time," and people kept bursting into song and jumping up to dance.

Gamma Molly pronounced it the best time she had ever had. Even Barbara was all smiles.

After dark, there was dancing and mingling in the great room. Dennis left Sharon's side occasionally to capture what he called "iconic" shots from the party.

What would become the most famous, the one displayed in people's homes for many years into the future, was of Finn and Gordie, in their shirt sleeves, ties loosened, sitting facing each other, in an interrupted conversation. Gabriel sat on his grandfather's knee, his arms outstretched toward his father who returned his delighted grin.

Molly called it the "three-peas-in-a-pod" picture.

As it got late, Gordie jumped up and grabbed Theresa's hand. "Come on, baby. Here's our song!"

Gordie was a wonderful dancer, and Theresa trusted him so completely that she could follow him anywhere he led. She said she could feel his energy through his hand on her back.

The beautiful couple gazed into each other's eyes. "I want to make love to you all night long, *T*," he told her softly.

"Oh, Gordie, please do," she whispered. "When can we start?"

"Very soon," he promised and led her off the floor as the song ended.

"Mommy, Daddy, guess what," said Gabriel excitedly. He was up far past his bedtime and was a little hyper. "Billy said I could sleep over with you! Isn't that great?"

"That's wonderful news, Buddy, and I would like to thank Billy very much," said Gordie dryly. Theresa and Kim laughed.

"I hope you have a real good night, Gordie," Billy said with mock sincerity. "The other kids are a little disappointed they can't stay too, but you do have Joy to take care of."

"Always thinking of others is our Billy," Kim poked him with her elbow.

"We'll see you late morning."

"What an absolutely fabulous time," were Theresa's last words as she snuggled up beside her husband.

In the morning, Gordie went to shower and was surprised when Gabriel asked if he could come in too. "We can sing," he suggested cheerily.

"Sure," said his father. "What would you like to sing?"

"*O Canada*," responded the little boy.

"Okay," Gordie said, "I'll wash your hair while we sing."

Gordie's big voice and Gabriel's little one resonated in the excellent acoustics of the shower. It was truly inspiring. Theresa lay in bed with her baby and thought her heart might explode with love. She knew she would remember this moment all her life.

May 2008

"Do you think we should do something about Mother's seventieth birthday?" Katherine asked Emma.

"I don't know," her sister replied. "She's been in an awful bad mood lately, saying stuff like 'Seventy years old and less than twenty years of happiness. I wish I'd gone to Fredericton with your father and been riding on the back of his snowmobile.'"

"Jesus," Kathy said. "I feel sorry for you, living with all that misery. As if you haven't had enough of your own.

"June 1 is a Sunday, and Eddie suggested that we take her to Lee's in Mount Hope the day before her birthday. She likes it there and hasn't been in a long while. He said we could book a room and have everybody there to surprise her. Just the immediate family plus Finn and Molly, of course.

"What do you think about that?"

"I think it sounds really nice. Eddie is the best, you know."

"I am well aware – and extremely grateful. I'll tell him yes and start communicating with everyone. I think it should work out well. Here's hoping there's no problem with Theresa and Gordie."

Everyone could make it, and Katherine and Eddie bullied Barbara into coming out for a change and stop being an old grouch. Barbara sort of took pride in being a grouch, but she didn't want to be an old one. And she did enjoy the Chinese food at Lee's.

There were twenty-nine guests, including grandchildren and great-grandchildren to surprise her. During the cocktail time, Barbara looked around the room and felt quite touched.

Her son David was arriving late, having had to finish something at work. When he came through the door, he clapped his hands to get everyone's attention. "And here is Mother's special birthday surprise," he announced. His brother Nicholas was with him.

Nicholas hadn't seen his mother since September 1974, almost thirty-four years ago. He was shocked by her appearance. Her pain and suffering were etched on her face.

He flashed back on their happy family times: Barbara sitting on Michael's lap singing *You Are My Sunshine*, the crochet tournaments when Grandpa always cheated, volleyball in the big pool, Barbara's loving kisses and hugs when someone got an "ouchy." That was what he wanted to remember.

"Momma," he said and took her in his arms. Barbara was as white as a sheet, and Eddie and Kathy stood close on each side. "Where have you been, boy?" she asked shakily. "You're almost late for dinner."

It was a rowdy good time. "When's everybody going to start crying?" Liam whispered to Alex.

"It could have happened when Uncle Nicholas got here, but Gran don't stand for no nonsense," his brother figured.

Late that night, after everyone had gone to bed at Maple Lane, Nicholas moved quietly through the halls and up to the third floor. Emma was sitting on her bed wearing a long sleeved white nightgown. Her hair was down. The drapes were open and the room was bright with moonlight. She looked like an angel.

"I knew you'd come," she said.

"Em… I…it…" he stammered. "Thirty-four years without you. I longed for you every day. I didn't come because I had promised God," he said.

"I know," she said. "I'm sorry your wife died."

"She was a good person, Em. I married her because I was so lonely and I missed you so much. She knew the whole time that I didn't love her, but she loved me anyway.

"Our sons are fine boys, but they hated the ranch and joined the armed forces. One's in Halifax and the other in Vancouver, so I am all alone again."

"My boys are good too. It's quite a miracle considering everything. Billy is my gift from heaven. I'm so lucky to have him near."

"Emmy, I think we've suffered enough. All of us. I want you to come home and live with me."

"How can we do that, Nicky?"

"We'll just say that you are coming for a holiday, and then you will decide to stay…if you want to."

"How can we explain our relationship to people?"

"In public, you will be my loved and trusted sister, my housekeeper, and hostess. In private, you will be my other half."

"What about God?"

"I've kept my promise to God for thirty-four years. I'll not live the rest of my life without you by my side."

"I'm afraid, Nicky."

"No, you're not, and you'll never be afraid again."

Everyone was happy to see Emma go home with Nicholas for a stay on the ranch. Unfortunately, Barbara was now left alone which was not a good thing.

Her children had to make an effort, and they did. Gabriel, not surprisingly, was her faithful comrade. Most afternoons he would have the school bus drop him off at Maple Lane for a visit.

There was always something to do. Sometimes they would go for a walk or they would have tea. They liked to go down to Cousin Todd's for a chat and to see the horses. Holiday season meant that presents had to be wrapped, and Gabriel would help bring decorations out of storage so they could plan for the open house.

These activities kept Barbara sober, and the whole family was grateful. Barbara actually flourished and ventured out in her car to go to Chamber of Commerce meetings and do chores. Of course, most times she drove Gabriel home and would often stay for dinner at Billy's. Billy was her boy, and Kim had been her best friend for years.

The other family members, Finn and Molly too, would come around on the weekends, and she flew to Antigonish a couple of times. She actually thought a number of times that she was glad she hadn't died with Michael in 1973.

As Thanksgiving 2010 approached, Barbara and Gabriel were planning her Thanksgiving family dinner. Gabriel was in the Arts Club at school and planned on making a centerpiece that he could submit as a project and use on the dinner table for the holiday.

Gabriel knew where to find the very best leaves, and he and Barbara went out to forage at the old Presbyterian Church.

They got loads of beautiful maple leaves and ran into the Pastor. He and Gabriel were great friends, and he got to hear all about the project.

He made some helpful suggestions, and Gabriel went home to get started. “Keep me updated,” Reverend Morwood called as Gabriel and Barbara walked away hand in hand.

Gallagher, Gabriel Finnegan

Suddenly, early Sunday, October 3, 2010, Gabriel Finnegan, "almost ten" years old, slipped away to reunite with the other angels. He leaves behind his heartbroken family.

Precious child of Gordon and Theresa Gallagher. Deeply loved by William Campbell Sheehan and Kimberly Scott (his second parents). Cherished grandson and great-grandson of Finnegan and Mary Margaret Gallagher and Barbara Campbell.

Adored brother of Mary Margaret, Michael-Gordon, Joy and Sean Gallagher and Alexander and William Sheehan.

Beloved nephew and great-nephew of Patrick and Linda Gallagher, Dennis and Sharon Gallagher, Shannon Gallagher and Philip Andrews, Erin Gallagher, and his special companion Mary Francis Gallagher; David and Susan Campbell, Nicholas Campbell, Emmalise Sheehan, and Katherine Campbell (Edward Gascoyne)

Gabriel was a remarkable little boy, loved by everyone who met him from the time of his birth. He was happy in Grade Four at Lake Avenue Elementary School where he was a member of the Arts Club and sang in the choir. Donations to the School in his memory would be greatly appreciated. A gathering to remember Gabriel will be held at 1:00 p.m. on Thursday, October 7 at St. Paul's Presbyterian Church in Dunnville.

Good afternoon, friends. Thank you for coming to join together to remember Gabriel. I am his uncle, Dennis Gallagher.

My wife is skeptical that I can do this. But I know I can. I can feel Gabriel's tiny hand in mine, and I will prevail.

Gabriel was a wise man disguised as a little boy. He had memories that stretched far into the past and visions of the future that were difficult for the rest of us to understand. My father, his beloved Gampa, believed that was because he was Irish, but so are we all. Gabriel was a seer.

He was precociously verbal, speaking as an adult at a very early age. Sometimes it was startling, other times hilarious. The pictures in his head were simple yet multi-layered. I would ask him philosophical questions just to be dazzled by his responses.

When his second sister was born, his parents asked him to suggest a name. He promptly replied, "Kitten Flower." The tiny girl was the size of a kitten and looked like a beautiful flower, so his response was perfect. To his parents' credit, that child's name is Barbara Joy Kitten Flower Gallagher.

When his baby brother arrived, Gordie and Theresa asked him about their choice of Sean Dennis, which is my name in reverse. Gabriel approved and said that name sounded very mature. I was proud because maturity is my eternal quest. Just ask my wife.

He was indiscriminately affectionate. Every occasion was a love fest. Everyone felt special after a kiss and hug from that busy little boy. He once told me that grumpy people just need more hugs. I've seen it work, and I urge you to remember.

Oh, for just one more hug from our beloved Gabriel.

Ladies and gentlemen: I am Edward Gascoyne. My wife is Katherine Campbell, which makes me great-uncle to our Gabriel.

I live in Vancouver and, unfortunately, do not spend as much time in Ontario as I should. However, I knew Gabriel well. We were great friends and enjoyed many a confidential conversation.

He was a young man who found many diverse things to be interesting. He liked to have me explain international politics to him, and he really enjoyed listening to me speak French. He thought it was cool that I call my wife "Kat." I think that was connected to his enormous love of animals, all living creatures, in fact.

I remember his inadvertently terrifying his sister, the gentle Molly, with a truly horrible spider he had found in the rocks up at South Cayuga. He just wanted to explain the amazing qualities of arachnids to her. Although I am not a fan, he talked to me and convinced me to let it walk on my arm. I don't want to do that again, but his knowledge impressed me as did his salesmanship abilities.

Afterward, I thought I should remember this incident and get him into sales in my corporation. But, alas, I recognized that he would probably give everything away to anyone whose personal story touched him. His heart was that big.

The last couple of days, I have walked about the town, talking to people about Gabriel. The response was universal: his generous spirit and bright curiosity about everything made him loved by everyone who met him.

I asked my wife, who is a very wise woman, how this could be. She looked at me and said simply, "He was an angel." I cannot dispute that. And I find it comforting because it makes me believe that he is here with us now and will be as long as we live.

A bientot, Gabriel. Nous t'aimons.

Good afternoon. I am Jennifer McCready, and I teach Grade Four at Lake Avenue Elementary School. I was Gabriel's homeroom teacher this year, but I met him last year when he joined the choir. He loved the choir and gave it his all. He inspired the other members and made each practice a lot of fun.

My outstanding memory of Gabriel is of his kindness. Early in September, I was very depressed when I came to school one day, but I put on my cheeriest professional face.

When we were alone, Gabriel asked me why I was sad, and I told him that my cat had died the previous day. He listened quietly and gave me a hug. Later, in the afternoon, I found a sympathy card on my chair. Gabriel had made it on his lunch hour.

That little boy showed me more kindness and empathy than my grown-up friends did, and I loved him for it.

His friends in the choir and I would like to honor him now with one of his favorite songs. We practiced this one really hard for the Spring Festival, but Gabriel loved it so much that he still asked to sing it on a regular basis, although the season had changed.

Ladies and gentlemen, please remember our good friend as you listen to *When the Red, Red Robin Comes Bob Bob Bobbin' Along*.

Oh, no, thought Kim, *not The Red, Red Robin*. She had heard the song a hundred times: Gabriel's pure soprano, Billy's bass, Molly's chirping and M-G's croaking. The song brought out the worst in Alex and Liam who added their *sotto voce* smutty lyrics, invariably causing Billy to make them run giggling from the room.

She snuck a peek down the pew at Billy who looked very grim. Alex and Liam were hanging their heads in shame. As well they should.

The dear little choir members sang with gusto, although it must have been hard. And everyone got through it.

You all know me, my friends. I am Ben Morwood, Pastor of this lovely church. Welcome to this blessed occasion.

Our dear Gabriel was not a member of our congregation, but he came to visit me regularly. He loved everything about the church – its classic architecture and its beautiful interior. He was particularly fascinated by the old gravestones of our early parishioners and would sit on the bench under the giant chestnut tree and commune with the departed.

I don't know exactly the nature of those conversations, but he did tell me that they were very happy to have such a wonderful resting place. I believed him. There just didn't seem to be any reason not to.

The last time I saw Gabriel was last Saturday. He was with his grandmother, Barbara, and they were collecting maple leaves for a Thanksgiving centerpiece he was creating. The summer weather had been such that the leaves were truly gorgeous, flawless, bright red beauties.

Gabriel was uncertain about the direction the project should take, and I suggested that if he worked with some white button chrysanthemums, he could make a Canadian flag.

I was hugged and pronounced a genius. I was proud. He promised to see me later in the week to let me know how things were progressing. Tragically, the next day didn't come for the wee boy.

My heart goes out to his devastated family. The ways of the Lord are sometimes hard to understand. What isn't hard to understand is that Gabriel, who was "almost ten," made a greater impact on the world around him and inspired more love and kindness than many who have opportunities far beyond their allotted "three score years and ten."

We love ye, Laddie. Until we meet again.

Hello. I am Mary Frances Gallagher. Gabriel was my nephew and my very best friend.

Just after he has born, Gabriel and his family came to live at my parents' home. He couldn't talk, of course, but it didn't matter. We were able to read each other's minds.

My daddy, who is Irish and quite mystical, although he won't admit it, called us "the faeries" and said we had our own language. We did, and we talked about everything.

We wondered what we were supposed to do in the world, and Gabriel always said we were meant to help each other. He didn't just mean other people; he meant animals too and the world itself. Of course he was right.

From the time he was small, Gabriel wanted to be a vet. However, in the last few months, he had been reconsidering that. He seemed to have reached a decision because, a short time ago, he said to me, "Mary Frances, I believe I should become a medical doctor because I think human beings need me more." I thought so too.

It was not to be this time around. Maybe on your next assignment, Gabriel.

As Mary Frances returned to her seat, the only sound was Finn sobbing. He was bent forward, his forehead resting on the pew in front of him. Molly cradled him in her arms, her face impassive. The rest of the family was completely undone by the sight of their broken patriarch, and many wept uncontrollably.

The only ones to maintain their composure were Molly and Mary Frances and Gordie and Theresa who sat like statues, tightly clasping each other's hand.

Poor Miss McCready rose to announce the closing musical offering. She spoke bravely although very slowly. "This is our last song for Gabriel. It was his favorite in the world. Please rise and join the choir in our national anthem *O Canada*."

The choir rose to their feet. Each child had a tiny Canadian flag. The assembled group stood, and the song began.

It was a very shaky start, the little voices quavering, the grown-up voices weakly joining in. Suddenly, a strong, clear voice took the lead. It was Gordie. The others took heart and soon the church rang with the triumphant song, celebrating our country and the little boy who loved it.

When it was over, Gordie embraced Theresa. Suddenly, Finn reached forward from the pew behind and gently stroked his sleeve. Gordie turned, and he reached out his hand. Finn held it in both of his. Their eyes locked briefly before Mary Frances and Molly led him out of the pew.

Gordie felt his knees weaken. "Come on, baby," Theresa said. "We've still got a ways to go." And he leaned on her as they left the church.

Gabriel's Miracles

Billy and Gordie stepped out of the crowded tea and cookies reception at the school auditorium. Both were looking more solid, but Billy obviously had something on his mind.

"Gordie, things have been better between us the last few years, but I want to say I'm sorry for being such an asshole for, you know, a long time. I understand that it wasn't your fault; it was just like a teenage dream in my head that I couldn't shake. I really want us to be friends."

"Forget about it, Billy," Gordie said. "I hope we can be brothers," and he held out his hand. Billy shook it warmly and continued somewhat hesitantly. "I want to ask your help."

"Anything," Gordie said.

"I want you and Theresa to help me get Kim to marry me." Billy looked embarrassed.

"What?" Gordie asked in surprise.

"Well, you know Kim came here from Toronto where she had a big-time job with that fancy hair stylist to the rich and famous Alexander Wolf. They were best friends and when he died he left her his Yorkville salon and more because she had been so good to him when he was sick.

"She hated that Toronto scene because she blamed it for his death. He had lived in the extremely fast lane. So she found a little beauty parlor on King Street where the owner was retiring. She worked there for a while, getting to know people, connecting, like that. That's how she met Gran.

"After people were used to her, she bought the old Russell place and renovated it into a real nice salon. At the end of 1994, she asked me if I would paint for her between Christmas and New Years before I was heading to Florida.

"It turned out to be a good opportunity in more ways than one. She had been thinking a lot about having a baby, and she talked about it with Gran. Gran told her to go ahead and seduce me. So she did.

"She was thirty-eight, a good-looking and sophisticated woman, and we did some powerful decorating. Come the New Year, off I went, never realizing that I had been used. I came back in June, none the wiser.

"Remember when I saw you and Teri at the beach and she said I'd do well to come home and catch up on all the news? I did and was mightily surprised. Kim told me not to worry about anything; she wanted nothing more from me. However, we had kind of become buddies so I saw a lot of her, and then Alex was born.

"I was totally crazy about the kid," he confessed.

"I remember," laughed Gordie. "At Barbara's Christmas Open House you wouldn't let anyone touch him 'cause of the germs."

"Yeah, well, you know how it is. Anyway, Kimmie wanted another baby really soon. She wanted them to be close in age so they could be tight friends. I agreed. We were totally on the same page.

"She asked nothing from me and allowed me complete access. The only thing she did say was to please not let them get close to me and then walk away from them. That wasn't going to happen, and I wasn't leaving her either.

"She became the best friend I've ever had. She encouraged me in every way and paid for me to go to school. She knows how much I hate to ask Gran for anything. She staked me on my house and helped me get my business off the ground. She loves our children and is bringing them up great, although they're a handful.

"Over the years, I've begged her to marry me, but she won't. She says the age difference is humiliating, and she says she won't tie me to an old woman.

"Gabriel was my confidant. He hoped more than anything that she would eventually say yes. Now he's gone, and I don't know what to do. Can you and Theresa help me?"

"Well," Gordie pondered. "Can't you say that this is just stupid since you intend to be with her to the end anyway? You could say that you won't tell anyone, and it'll be a romantic secret between the two of you, nobody else knowing. Women love stuff like that.

"And you should get her now when she's in a weakened condition and say that it will make Gabriel really, really happy."

"Genius," said Billy.

"Listen," said Gordie, "I'm an ex-con, and apparently we're all masters of manipulation." That struck them both as funny, and they laughed together for the first time ever.

"If this works out," said Billy, "I'm going to do something really special for you."

"You already have, Billy. You already have."

"You are a magnificent man, Gascoyne," Katherine said, tip-toeing her fingers across his chest.

"Why, thank you, my baby kitten. Does that mean you are willing to share yourself with me again?"

Eddie typically called her "Kat," using diminutives such as "my baby kitten" when he was relaxed and amorous. At the height of passion, he would often lapse into his mother tongue which always thrilled her. The electricity between them had lasted for thirty years since they had first laid eyes on each other on a snowy day in Winnipeg.

The details of that meeting were fuzzy. Nobody knew what had really happened. The story for public consumption was that Katherine, on her way on the bus to her uncle's ranch in Edmonton, had temporarily taken a job in a bar in Winnipeg. Eddie was a traveling salesman of bar-related items.

That was sort of true. Actually, she was working as a topless waitress in Winnipeg's biggest strip club. When Eddie first saw her, she was wearing stiletto heels, tiny sequined hot pants, and not another stitch. She had long red hair, gathered up, and he thought she was the most astonishingly beautiful girl he had ever seen.

"Forget about her," his friend Jim, the bar manager, said. "The chick's like a robot. She just comes to work and leaves immediately after. Always looks like she's got something on her mind."

Eddie was a determined person whose mission was now crystal clear. On her break, he made her talk to him. She was the smartest and strongest girl he had ever met.

He was also a person who usually got what he wanted, and when he left Winnipeg a few days later, he took her with him.

As they drove out of town, Katherine asked him how Jim had taken the news. "Just like I knew he would," Eddie laughed. "He called me a fucking bastard and a son of a bitch."

"I hope he didn't hurt your feelings," she joked.

"Are you kidding? He made me feel like a king!"

Eddie was ambitious. He had plans which he decided to pursue now that he had won the heart of the crown jewel of all women. He gave up his sales job, which had served him well, and got involved in the bar/restaurant business in Vancouver. There was a ton of money to be made.

And he did. He was a millionaire by the time he was thirty. On this particular night when he lay in bed with Katherine, he was worth a fortune. He had worked hard, obsessively, and it had cost him a great deal over the years. His marriage, although unorthodox, worked. And that was, in the final analysis, what mattered most to him. He adored his Kat.

Their two children were very bright and successful in their chosen fields but low-key and modest in spite of their father's wealth. The time had come for the change Eddie had been contemplating for some time. The death of Gabriel seemed to cause things to gel for him.

He wondered if it was the early onset of Alzheimer's that had made the old Beatles' song *All You Need is Love* play constantly in his head for the last few days. He was prepared to admit that it might be true – if you've got a security net of a few million dollars.

Eddie and Katherine had a good deal more than a few million dollars, and he wanted to talk specifics with her. He missed her and wanted to liquidate his Vancouver assets and come back to Ontario to be with her until the end of his life.

The loss of Gabriel emphasized the capriciousness of fate. In the wink of an eye, either one of them could be gone. The very idea of losing her made him feel frightened and weak. He wanted to move forward as quickly as he could.

"What a worried frown! Whatever are you thinking about, darling," Katherine asked.

"Of course I want to share with you. But first, I want to tell you how proud you made me today at the church. Everything you said was perfect. Especially the part about my being wise," and she nibbled on his shoulder.

"I was just grateful that the church's roof didn't collapse when we walked in," Eddie said.

"We are a bad lot, aren't we?" his wife laughed.

"Dennis, baby, maybe you would feel better if you could just stop crying and talk to me," Sharon said with concern. "Please try and tell me what you and Eddie and Gordie and Billy were talking about this evening."

She sat down on the bed and he put his head in her lap. He was hot and gulping like a heartbroken child. She petted him gently and coaxed him to tell her everything.

"Eddie's coming to Ontario as soon as possible. He doesn't want to be away from Kathy any more. But he has to sell off out there, which means he will have major cash to work with. Of course, there will be huge taxes and all that stuff I don't understand.

"He suggested setting up a foundation in Gabriel's memory, using a bunch of his money to get started. We all liked that but didn't know what. Billy kind of thought that it should be an ongoing thing instead of a scholarship fund which only happens once or twice a year. And visible instead of just giving money to Mac Medical Center or something.

"Maybe like The Children's Wish, kind of, but for everyone, even animals. People make requests which a board would consider and accept or reject. Anyway, it would take a lot of work to set it up, and we'd have to get licenses and so on. We'd have to develop policies and procedures and promote it. We'd have to appoint people we trust to various roles.

"It's all really complicated, Sharona, and too hard for me. Eddie said it would take a long time to pull it together. We would have to move ahead patiently and carefully, trying it keep it in the family if possible.

"That's all I can tell you; it makes my brain hurt. Eddie did say that something extremely important would be a promotional video about Gabriel. I said I could do that. I have lots of footage I could use."

God bless Eddie, Sharon thought. He knew exactly the right thing to suggest to Din, something really meaningful that her gentle, artistic husband could immerse himself in.

"I think it's a wonderful beginning," she said soothingly. "Gabriel must be so proud. Eddie's right in that every step has to be taken with the utmost deliberation. But you don't have to think about any of that, sweetheart. Just think about the video."

"Now, don't you feel a little bit better?" she asked kindly. "Why don't I bring us some hot chocolate, and then we can cuddle?"

Gordie climbed the stairs to the bedroom. He moved very slowly. This day had been so long that he couldn't remember any day before it. Tomorrow he and Theresa would fly home to Antigonish, to their small children. He couldn't remember what they looked like.

In the bedroom, by the pale light of a small lamp, he could see his wife and older children asleep on the big bed. They were fully dressed, probably having fallen asleep while talking, trying to comfort each other.

He looked at them: Theresa, his heart, his life; his son and daughter, poor kids, shell-shocked by the loss of their tiny leader. How were they all to carry on?

He was overcome by exhaustion and gently lay down on his side next to Molly. He put his arm across her protectively, and she stirred and turned toward him. She sleepily opened her eyes and looked at him. "Daddy," she murmured and smiled sweetly before dropping off again.

At that moment, Gordie chose to believe that ultimately everything would be okay, and he fell into a dreamless sleep.

Back in Antigonish, Gordie and Theresa were welcomed with open arms. Their friends and relatives shared their grief at the loss of their dear little boy and did everything they could to help the couple cope.

It seemed a long wait for the coroner's report following Gabriel's autopsy. Gordie was very quiet and unlike himself. Theresa knew that he was afraid that Gabriel's premature birth might have been a contributing factor. She was worried too.

The report eventually arrived. Gabriel had been in perfect health. He was a small child, but his organs were proportionately sized. There was no apparent reason for him to die. He had no history of sleep apnea or any other problem. He had just gone away in the night.

Mary Francis felt that it wasn't like Gabriel to go and leave his Thanksgiving project unfinished. She could suppose nothing other than he had to answer a call, but she was sure he was with them all.

Gordie was relieved, but his heart ached. He threw himself into his work which forced him to be outgoing and cheerful. At home, he and Theresa clung to each other and their two little children.

Finn seemed to have aged ten years. It was time for him to retire, but he stayed on at the steel company on a contract basis. He too sought refuge in work and in Molly's arms. Molly kept busy with her various good works, but as always Finn was her life.

Billy and Kim and the four remaining children suffered the most, living every day without Gabriel. With the resilience of children, the kids returned to their school and routines. But it wasn't the same, and it never would be.

Something good did happen. Kim agreed to marry Billy, and she said it didn't have to be a secret. She agreed that they loved each other and should make the most of every day. All the children were delighted.

At the beginning of December, Billy, Kim, and the children traveled on a weekend to Antigonish to stay with the Gallaghers. Gordie had arranged for a Justice of the Peace to perform the ceremony at their house, and Theresa planned a wonderful dinner to follow. After dinner, in time for the cutting of the cake, Seamus and his brood of O'Connors came over to celebrate.

They sang and danced to Irish songs and toasted with Irish whiskey until late.

"I feel truly married," said Kim, and she kissed Billy.

"Brother," said Billy, putting his arm around Gordie, "I have you and Gabriel to thank for this day. You encouraged me, and Gabriel was rooting for me. I promised you a gift if this happened, and I will keep my word."

After everyone had gone home, Billy said to his bride, "Come on, Kimmie. Let's go upstairs and consummate our marriage."

Kim laughed and looked at Alex and Liam who were sound asleep on the couch and said, "I think we've already done that."

Upstairs in the guest bedroom which Theresa and Molly had turned into a bridal suite, Billy pulled Kim over to the window. It was a very blustery night, and Billy said, "This is like the night we made Alex."

"We could have made him any one of a dozen or more times over those two days," Kim reminded him.

"I had never been so turned on in my life," Billy admitted.

"You were a stallion," his wife caressed his cheek.

"I have something for you," he said, reaching into his pants pocket. He pulled out a ring and slid it onto her finger over the wedding band he had given her earlier that day. It was a sapphire with a diamond on each side.

"This is you," he said, indicating the sapphire. "And these are our sons."

Billy wasn't predisposed to emotional displays or sentimentality. In the past, he had given her gifts like a toaster oven or a new sink for the powder room. He rarely expressed his feelings in such plain language. Kim burst into tears.

"Kimberly," he said. "You are the best thing that ever happened to me, and I love you with all my heart."

Now was the time to consummate their marriage.

The family gathered at Barbara's on Christmas Eve. Everyone was filled with dread, but they did have Billy and Kim's marriage to celebrate and the new house that Dennis and Sharon were having built.

This year, there was no open house. Barbara just wasn't up to it. But she had a nice tree and a festive meal catered for thirty. She rose to announce dessert. "It might be a strange thing to announce dessert," she said. "But this is special for our beloved boy. I know that he is here, and he will love it."

The lights were lowered, and dessert carts were rolled out into the Great Room from two directions, decorated with dozens and dozens of fairy lights. The effect was stunning. The children squealed with delight, and the adults cheered and applauded. They all knew that Gabriel was thrilled.

On Christmas Day, Gordie, Theresa, Joy, and Sean went to dinner and to stay overnight at Finn and Molly's. That night, when the four adults were alone, Theresa spoke.

"This might not be the best time, or maybe it is the perfect time. But we have something for you.

"We love you more than we can describe, and we know that Gabriel did too. We want you to have one third of his ashes to do with as your hearts dictate.

"Please try to rejoice in this last gift he has left for us. I hope you will eventually decide on something that will bring you and him peace and joy."

Theresa smiled and placed the small wooden box on the table. She rose and kissed her in-laws and sat back down beside Gordie who pulled her into his arms. "Well put, my baby," he said to her. "I couldn't do it," he admitted to his parents.

A similar scene was enacted the next morning at Billy and Kim's before Gordie and Theresa flew back to Antigonish. Billy took it very hard and cried like a child.

"He'll be fine," Kim promised. "He keeps things bottled up so, but the wedding was a great diversion for us. We both can never thank you enough for your role in that and for including us this way.

"We were planning on asking you if we could all come to visit on the March Break before Billy gets busy." Of course they could. They would meet again when the long winter ended.

Gordie didn't think anything more about Billy's promise of a gift until after the Scott-Sheehans' March Break visit when a big truck and backhoe arrived in front of his house. They were there to plant a young maple tree on his front lawn. He was handed an envelope, and the enclosed note said:

Dear Gordie. Here it is at last. My thank you for your friendship through the toughest time imaginable and the happiest day of my life. See you soon. Billy.

Billy and his family didn't know what to do about Gabriel's ashes.

One evening, over dinner, out of nowhere, Alex said, "Niagara Falls."

And Liam said, "On Canada Day."

This was commonplace. One would have a thought immediately followed up by the other. They typically finished each other's sentences.

"At night," said Alex.

"When the lights are on," finished Liam.

M-G, who wasn't much of a talker, said, "Cool." Molly agreed.

All Billy could think about was Niagara Falls on Canada Day, and his enthusiasm level wasn't that high, although he could see that it was a perfect idea. "How about we go there in the middle of the night?" he suggested. "Then we will have more privacy and be able to get right to the edge of the Falls?"

That idea was applauded as even cooler, thank God. It was a plan.

Everything went smoothly. It was a beautiful night with more people around than you'd think, but they got to the edge and scattered the ashes over the thundering Falls.

"We love you, Gabriel," called Alex.

"Don't forget us," said Liam.

M-G looked up at Billy. “My brother,” he said, and Billy put one arm around him and the other around Molly.

Kim, who had been terrified that they would all be arrested for littering or some such, said, “Let’s go to that all-night place we saw on the way in where they have maple leaf ice cream cakes.” She was declared the smartest mom ever.

Theresa and Gordie had also had many long conversations about Gabriel’s ashes. Finally, they decided to go to Murray Beach in New Brunswick. Theresa commented that the name Murray made it all the more appropriate.

It was a wonderful provincial park where their family had camped a number of times, enjoying the long white beach on the Northumberland Strait. The water was warm and shallow so it was a safe place for the children. The kids loved it, and the family would travel into Shediac at least once each visit to enjoy the lobster dinner laid out every night.

Gabriel would come home brown as a berry and full of tales of the sand critters and the new friends he had made and anything else that caught his fancy that trip.

It was a great playground for their angel.

In August, Molly and M-G flew down, and the family headed to Murray Beach.

They got up before sunrise and walked down to the beach. The tide was some distance out. Gordie, using Gabriel’s bright yellow beach shovel, dug a place for his son’s ashes. The family stood in a circle until the water had risen to their ankles and the sun was pink streaks. The little mound of sand and Gabriel were gone.

“Let’s go and have a real Canadian breakfast, kids,” said Theresa in the most cheerful voice she could muster. They had pancakes with fresh picked blueberries and maple syrup and Canadian bacon cooked on their Coleman stove and the campfire. It was delicious, and Gabriel would have loved it after his swim.

Gordie was at the stove, pouring himself a cup of coffee, when Molly came up and pressed her face against him. She was crying.

"Come on, Muffy, come walk with Daddy," he said, putting his arm around her.

They walked back to the beach and sat beside a sand dune. Gordie thought that she was upset about Gabriel, but it was something else. "I want to come and live here, Daddy," she said, "but I don't want to hurt Billy and Kim's feelings. I've been thinking about it since last summer when you and I walked around the university campus. I want to finish high school here and study music at St. Francis Xavier."

"Billy and Kim know that birds have to fly," said Gordie. "Alex will be going to university pretty soon, won't he? And he's thinking about living in Hamilton at Kathy and Eddie's?"

"Maybe. I don't see how he can part from Liam."

"These are the realities of life, baby. One day you will leave me and Mommy too. Do you want one or both of us to be with you when you talk to Kim and Billy?"

"No, thank you, Daddy. I have to do it myself. But please tell me what we are going to do about my piano?"

Gordie hugged her. "You just leave that to me. Billy and I will figure it out." They walked hand in hand back to the camp site.

Upon arrival, Gordie was greeted by his little son Sean. Sean was feeling sad and confused. He could barely remember his big brother Gabriel who had gone away without saying goodbye. He didn't really understand what they had done this morning, but he knew that his parents weren't quite the same as usual.

Sean loved Gordie more than anyone in the world, and he held out a somewhat grubby little hand. "Look, Daddy, I saved you the biggest blueberry."

Gordie picked him up and said, "That's very thoughtful of you, son. Why don't you pop it in my mouth?" Sean did, and Gordie kissed him.

Gordie looked at Theresa and saw the love in her eyes. He knew beyond any doubt that he was the luckiest man alive.

After the children were settled for the night, by the campfire, Theresa and Gordie talked about Molly's request. Of course they were overjoyed, but they felt bad for Billy and Kim who had done so much for their kids.

Although Molly had told Gordie that she would talk to them on her own, Gordie wondered if he should give Billy a heads-up. Maybe that would make it easier. Molly and M-G were flying home in two days. After long discussion, Molly's parents decided to respect their daughter's wishes and let her proceed as she wished.

The evening after the kids' departure, Billy phoned. He said that Molly had broken the news in the car on the way from the airport.

"God, I hope you're not bitter towards us because of this, Billy," said Gordie. "I know you'll miss her bad. And so soon after the loss of our baby."

"It is hard. Molly is our best girl," replied Billy, "but you are her parents. We are grateful that you shared her with us for eight years. At any time after you got settled in Antingonish, you could have taken all three of them back. But you didn't.

"You let them get used to you and introduced them to Antigonish and let them make their own decisions. I'm sorry you didn't have more time with Gabriel. Truly sorry.

"Molly said that you told her Kim and I would understand that birds got to fly, and we do. We've got two fledglings who will be on their way before too long.

"I guess we're grown-ups now, Gordie, and we have to face these things."

"Do you think we'll ever be as mature as Din," Gordie asked.

"Unlikely," Billy laughed. "We don't have Sharon on our asses."

Billy sat down to read his e-mails, and the first one almost jumped off the screen. It was from Gamma Molly, and though Billy didn't know how it was possible, it seemed to be vibrating with excitement. It read:

To our wonderful children

I'm sending this note because if I get on the phone, you know how I am. LOL

Eddie and Kathy are sending us to Ireland as a birthday gift to me. We will leave on the Labor Day Weekend and come back on Halloween. There is so much to do to get ready!!!

Fortunately, we have our passports from when Daddy wanted to go and see the Civil War battlefields three years ago. Whew!

We are traveling to and from Shannon – and wonderful Eddie booked us first class! I told Daddy we will be like a king and queen. We're going to stay with my family and at some point travel to Dublin to see Uncle Thomas and his new wife. I am attaching all the addresses and flight info.

We are taking our boy's ashes with us to scatter. I would like them to be scattered at Cobh where Daddy and I met and fell in love. Daddy agreed, but then he started to have "heritage" thoughts about the site of the beginning of the Rebellion in Dublin or William Butler Yeats' grave. Those are good choices, and you know that anything Daddy chooses is my favorite too.

Daddy doesn't think he wants to worry about his laptop, so we will be sure to take lots of photos to share when we get home – just in time for the arrival of our new grandchild!!!!!

I am so excited about everything that Daddy has to keep giving me big bear hugs so I don't float away! Be good children, and remember that we love you with all our hearts.

Mommy and Daddy

Billy was laughing so hard that he was holding his sides. "Come read this, Kimmie," he called. "It's just perfect."

"I'm so happy for them, Billy," Kim said. "I hope this will close one door and reopen some others for them."

"I wonder how many bear hugs Finn has had to give her so far today." Billy mused. "Too bad there aren't more than three choices for Gabriel's ashes. We could have had a pool."

"Gabriel would think that was really funny. What do you think they'll choose?" Kim asked.

"My money's on Cobh, although the Dublin Post Office is a big 'heritage' favorite."

"I think you're right." She rubbed his shoulders. "You're right so often, I can hardly stand it."

September 2011

Molly was happy. Her decision to move to Antigonish had been almost a year in the making. It had started when she and Gordie had gone for a walk on the grounds of St. Francis Xavier University in the summer of 2010. She was stimulated by the academic atmosphere, and she loved being with her father.

The seed was sown, and she sent away for a catalogue and other information about St Francis' music program. Molly was a talented pianist, and music was her dream.

And now she had arrived. She wanted to come early and finish high school there. From her visits to Antigonish, she knew a lot of kids at her high school, including many of her cousins. It was her intention to work as hard as she could and aim for a scholarship.

She missed everyone back home, Billy and Kim and her brothers especially, but she was overjoyed to be with her parents and little sister and brother.

Joy was five years old and a one-woman Molly fan club. She thought her big sister was amazing, and she wanted to be just like her in every way. She often coaxed Molly to fix her hair just like her own.

That was quite a challenge considering that Molly had her grandmother's wavy strawberry blond hair and Joy had inherited Finn and Gordie's straight black hair. Molly did her best, and when Joy proudly presented herself to Gordie, asking if she looked exactly like Molly, he said, "Well, Joyous, if I close my eyes, you are identical."

The sound of music filled the house. Barbara had hired professional movers to bring Molly's piano from Ontario. Joy would sit riveted, watching and listening for long stretches. She wanted to learn to play too.

Molly showed her some simple scales, and Joy was inspired. She practiced them until one of her parents would distract her with something else. Molly took her a little further with songs like *Frere Jacques* – that one was for Uncle Eddie. Joy could play it for him on Gran's piano at Christmas.

Molly loved her baby sister and was fascinated how she was progressing, being only five. "Mommy," Molly said, "I'm thinking maybe I would like to be a teacher."

"Piano teachers don't make very much money," Theresa said. "Maybe you could think about taking a Bachelor's in Education with a minor in music."

"I'm going to think about that." Molly replied. "I know I'm not talented enough to play professionally, and I think that life is grueling. Teaching music in the school system might be just perfect."

Gordie and Molly had a special relationship. Theresa often said that their daughter had imprinted on her father in the first few minutes of her life, and no man had ever loved his child more.

That night when Gordie was relaxing in the living room, she snuggled up next to him as she often did and told him about her conversation with Theresa. "I think it's an idea worth considering seriously, Muff," he said. "I've always said that your mother is much more than a beautiful face. And so are you."

November 2011

"Please come to our party on Saturday to see our new home and meet our new daughter. We are fully confident that you will be blown away. Not so much by the house, but by our little darling."

So began the invitation from Dennis and Sharon. All the family was planning on attending. Nobody knew the baby's name. On Saturday, she would be four days old.

Dennis greeted the guests and made them comfortable. They strolled around the stunning house that Dennis had helped design. When Alex and Liam had had enough suspense, they started a chant: “Baby, Baby, Baby!”

Dennis, who was so excited that his cheeks looked like Santa Claus’, laughed and called to Sharon to bring on the star of the show. The child was bundled in pink and white blankets, and no one could see her face.

“Daddy and Mommy, come up here,” Dennis said. “We want you to be the first ones to hold her.” And he placed her in Finn’s arms.

“Her name is Fawn Gabrielle.”

Finn pushed back the blankets and looked into Fawn’s wee face. She appeared to be considering him right back. He tenderly cupped her wispy little blonde head with his hand and whispered, “Our baby peach.”

Molly burst into tears, precipitating a flurry of tissues around the room. “Told ya,” said Alex to his brother.

January 2012

The year since Gabriel had died had been very hard for Barbara. The loss of her little friend had changed her life once again. The departure of Molly to live with her parents was another blow. She had enjoyed the couple of days a week Molly had come to visit and play her grand piano. Now Barbara was alone in the big house with nothing in particular to do or think about.

She didn’t want to revert to her old habits, but the crystal decanters on the buffet called to her. She resisted nobly, but there had been slip-ups. She decided to seek help, and she asked Eddie to come to visit her.

Eddie knew from personal experience that she had to expand her horizons, and they talked about options. Eddie had wanted her to get involved in building the Gabriel’s Miracles

Foundation, but getting that venture off the ground was proving to be complicated and time-consuming. Exactly what was going to happen was uncertain.

The two talked about Barbara's selling Maple Lane, since it wasn't an appropriate home for anyone in the family, and Barbara's moving into a seniors' residence. She couldn't bring herself to seriously consider that idea. Nor could she think about moving in with any of her children or grandchildren.

"Do you know of any other ladies who are alone?" Eddie asked. "Maybe you could take in a couple of companions, like on that television show *Golden Girls*."

"Maybe that's a good idea," Barbara said. "I believe I do know a couple of women who might be interested."

She and Eddie decided to do some brainstorming. Eddie typically carried a handheld recorder with him, and got it out. "Okay," he said, "I'll state a topic, and we'll toss ideas back and forth. Just ideas, not details."

And so they did: qualities of the candidates, modifications to the house, legal responsibilities, staffing needs, monthly fees, and so on. The ideas flew fast and furious. When they stopped, Barbara was breathless and exhilarated.

"Great start," Eddie exclaimed.

"So you should proceed like this: use these ideas to design a plan, talk it over with your lawyer, and then work on the details. There's no rush. You want this to be done right, and set it up so that you can terminate the arrangement, giving notice, of course, if you aren't happy."

Barbara had been contemplating, and she looked up and nodded. For the first time, Eddie caught a glimpse of the girl she had been. He had never noticed that she had beautiful hazel eyes like Theresa's. They were flashing with light and life.

"I will be talking to you regularly about this, if you don't mind," she said.

"It will be my pleasure," he replied as he got up and put on his coat.

"Now, you know, Barb," he said, putting his arm around her when they reached the door. "If it goes this way, you will have to be gracious and nice all the time. If you feel grouchy or bossy, you will have to retire to your quarters until you're in better spirits."

Barbara smiled at him and said, "I know," and her hazel eyes twinkled.

Easter 2012

For the long weekend, Theresa and Gordie and their children came to stay at Finn and Molly's. The family was coming, and Molly happily prepared dinner for twenty-five.

In the afternoon, Finn, Eddie, Billy, Gordie, Dennis, and their brother Pat met in Finn's office to talk about the Gabriel's Miracles Foundation. They were disappointed in their lack of progress but realized it was understandable. The suddenness of Gabriel's death and everyone's overwhelming grief afterwards had held the project back.

However, some steps had been taken. Patrick, who was a CPA, had seen to the paperwork necessary to register their idea as a charitable foundation.

Eddie had been working to liquidate his assets in Vancouver with as little fiscal pain as possible. He had formed a partnership with Larry his lawyer and best friend. He had downsized and sold off properties. He had transferred a great deal of the money to the Foundation. But they had to spend some of it on charitable causes.

His original plan was to hold an official meeting of the Foundation principals to appoint a Board of Directors who would vote Finn as Chairman. That just hadn't been possible, but Finn was feeling better. His trip to Ireland with Molly had invigorated him, and he was almost his old self.

He did declare that he didn't feel quite up to it right now, but soon.

Eddie had been thinking about what they could do immediately and suggested that they offer an annual full scholarship to the medical school at the University. The group could develop a list of criteria for potential recipients and contact the Development Office of the University.

He said that they could enter into discussions with the University about their proposal and work from there. Who would be the contact person?

Eddie was extremely busy and back and forth from Vancouver. Gordie said, "I'm not the one. I'm the guy who fixes their cars. Plus I live in Nova Scotia."

Billy said, "God, no. I can't do it. I'm the guy who mows their lawns." All eyes turned to Dennis.

Dennis had become much more mature, a lot of the time. He was a star at work, he was a father, and he was married to Sharon who was very strict. He admitted that he could do it. But he wanted to be introduced by a letter from Gordie who was Gabriel's father.

Everyone agreed. Such letter would be prepared.

The initial amount for discussion would be determined from the University's calendar. Billy said, "I wouldn't like this scholarship to be just about grades and possibly go to a kid from a wealthy family. It should go to someone who would have a tough time without it."

Everyone agreed.

By the time dinner was served, the guys felt great. They were moving ahead, and what could be a better time than Easter?

June 2013

Finn always called M-G a man of few words. They got along really well, going for long walks without speaking a word until they got home. Finn would usually say something like, "Good time, boy," and M-G would give him a hug. He loved his grandfather.

Although there was no one who would know it, M-G was the essence of Finn before he met Molly and turned into the person he was now.

M-G missed his sister and Gabriel a lot. They were the two people with whom he had always talked. He loved his mother, but he had been sorely hurt when she had abandoned her family to go with the unknown person. As he got older and saw his parents' deep love for each other, his heart softened, but in his mind, he always thought of his father as Gordie.

He had to admit that Gordie was good-natured and funny and pretty cool. When M-G was in Antigonish, he took him to the service center where he worked and showed him many interesting things and how they were used. M-G enjoyed thinking about that when he went to bed at night.

All that aside, M-G felt like his real home was with Billy and Kim and the guys. He felt close to Kim and considered Alex and Liam to be his brothers. He worshiped Billy and wanted to work with him when he finished school.

Just because M-G didn't say much didn't mean that he missed anything that was going on around him.

He was worried about his Dunnville family. Both boys wanted to study engineering, and Alex was going to university in September. Liam would follow in a year. That was a good thing except the brothers had never been apart. This was a great concern which wasn't discussed, but when Alex's upcoming departure was mentioned, M-G could see something like panic in the boys' eyes.

He worried about them a lot and wished he could help.

He took a few days in Antigonish in June to celebrate his fifteenth birthday, and he hoped he could talk to Molly or Theresa. Molly was busy so the opportunity was never there. He tried to talk to Theresa, but his little sister and brother were always interrupting. Before long, it was time for him to go home.

At breakfast on his last day, Gordie asked him if he would like to come to the service center and see a vintage Corvette Stingray an old guy was bringing in to show Gordie. Would he?! It was immaculate, perfect, the most beautiful car M-G had ever seen, and he was high as a kite as he and Gordie walked home.

In his euphoric state, M-G decided to take a shot and told Gordie what was on his mind. What did Gordie think?

Gordie figured it was a problem that could be easily solved. "When I met your mother," he said, "she was going to a fancy private school in Hamilton, and Sharon was going to a first-class high school.

"Alex is going to stay with Kathy and Eddie, isn't he? Well, I'd bet my last dollar that they would have Liam too, and he could go to that school. It would be a great wrap-up to his high school career, doing grade twelve at the top-ranked high school in Hamilton instead of Dunnville District High.

"Maybe you could talk to Billy about that."

M-G mulled that over. It seemed to be a great idea. He'd talk to Billy as soon as he got back.

As they walked up the sidewalk to the house, he looked up at Gordie and said, "Thanks, Daddy."

September 2013

It was hard to believe that Joy and Sean were seven and six years old, in Grades Two and One. Everybody was gone from home by 8:30, and Theresa felt kind of lonesome. She always had lots of work to do, and the highlight of her day was taking Gordie his lunch.

Gordie wanted to get her a dog, but they agreed that it wasn't fair to ask someone to look after their pet when they went away to Ontario several times a year. Gordie fretted about her, and suggested that she take some part-time university courses or consider volunteering somewhere.

University-level courses when she still had a large domestic load seemed too much for her, so she asked around about volunteering. The public library was always looking for help, and that seemed perfect.

Theresa started out with one afternoon a week and progressed to two. That was because the little kids in Junior Kindergarten and Kindergarten at the elementary school down the street walked to the library twice a month.

Naturally, Theresa was wonderful with the children, and soon she was reading and telling stories to them. They loved the Story Circle and Mrs. G. Sometimes, Gordie would briefly drop in with his acoustic guitar and sing them some songs. They initially called him "Mr. Gallagher," but he said that was his father – to great hilarity, the kids being too young to have heard that old joke before – so they called him Gordie, and they loved him and his music.

After school one library day, Kindergartener Julia Brown walked home with her mother, enthusing about what a good time it had been. “And you know, Mommy,” she observed, “every time Gordie leaves to go back to work, he kisses Mrs. G.”

Donna Brown smiled a little wistfully. “Everyone should know a love like the Gallaghers’, Jules,” she said.

Early March 2014

Eddie had a big soft spot for Theresa and Gordie.

When he came to Maple Lane in 1985, looking for Katherine, he had never been so nervous. When he pulled into the parking area, he saw her in front of the house with two little girls and a baby in her arms. He assumed the children were some of her nieces and nephews.

As he approached the group, the pounding of his heart drowned out his own voice as he greeted them. Katherine introduced the girls, and the really pretty one with the enormous eyes took a step forward. She looked up at him and said, “You’re gorgeous.” He chuckled, and the ice was broken.

Eddie considered that to be the greatest day of his life, reunited with his beloved Kat and meeting the son he didn’t know he had. In his memory, Theresa played a starring role.

Eddie was in full agreement with Gordie that their first child was indeed a little treasure. She looked like her grandmother and grew more and more like her as she got older. Eddie called her “*La P’tite,* Molly” and always made a special fuss over her.

When he heard about her audition at McGill in early March, he recognized the expense involved for Gordie and Theresa. He suggested to Katherine that they go to Antingonish and take Molly to Montreal for her audition. They could go the previous afternoon so that she could relax a little and bring her home after the audition was over.

Kathy thought it was a splendid idea. They could have a short visit with Gordie and Theresa, just the four of them, and spend some time with Molly.

Theresa and Gordie were very grateful, and Molly was beyond excited. Going to Montreal with Eddie and Kathy and the audition the next day was the biggest adventure of her life.

They stayed overnight in a suite in a hotel as elegant as anything Molly had ever seen in a magazine. The night before the audition, they had dinner at a five-star restaurant in the Old Town, and Eddie ordered all kinds of special things. He spoke French to everyone, and Molly felt like a princess in such sophisticated company.

Down to earth the next day, she attended the audition. She knew high school French, and Eddie had coached her as to a gracious greeting to the judicators.

Hello, friend, she thought as she sat down at the grand piano, and she began her two pieces, one chosen by the University's Music Department, the other her own selection. She felt wonderful and played flawlessly.

The judges kept poker faces as they thanked her and indicated that she would receive word within ten days to two weeks. After she left the room, they smiled at each other. Not only was she a talented pianist, but an adorable young girl with her sweet greeting and becoming white dress embroidered with tiny shamrocks (a gift from Gordie who had made a special trip to Halifax).

Ten long days passed before the acceptance letter from McGill arrived, followed the very next day by good news from St. Francis Xavier. Molly was walking on clouds, and her parents felt about to burst with pride.

It was a hard choice. Molly asked Theresa for her opinion. Theresa didn't want to influence her, but she did say that living in Montreal would be a wonderful experience, and Molly would be completely bilingual when she graduated.

Gordie put his arms around her and said, "Follow your heart, baby."

There was no question where her heart lay – in Antigonish with her parents and little sister and brother. Gordie advised her not to be hasty and take a couple of days to decide.

Another consideration was that St. Francis Xavier University provides students entering from high school with a grade point average of at least eighty-five percent with a $5,000 scholarship. Molly easily met that requirement, and her choice was made.

September 2014

It was an exciting time. Molly was starting university. She wasn't nervous, just hungry for learning and the new people she would meet. "I can't wait," had been her mantra for several months.

Her parents never let on, but they were overwhelmed with relief that she would be studying in Antigonish and living at home. Theresa had been sure her heart would break if her little girl were over seven hundred miles away, and Gordie had stewed over the terrible things that could happen to his baby in the big city. Now they could relax for a few more years.

Summer 2015

Katherine never walked in downtown Hamilton unless it was at the busiest times of day. Although some areas were struggling to make a comeback, most of it was rundown and sleazy.

Panhandlers and people lying on the sidewalk were common. The eastern section was particularly seedy, and Katherine had to walk there on this particular day to look at a property on Eddie's behalf. Some optimistic developers were trying to convert what had been, in a previous life, a luxury hotel into condos. Kathy asked herself who the hell would want to come home after dark in this neighborhood.

As she stepped off the curb to cross the street, a woman from the other direction literally bumped into her. Kathy pulled her purse close to her body and moved away.

"Kathy," the woman said softly. Kathy took a look and recognized her sister Caroline.

No one knew anything about Caroline's whereabouts. About ten years previous, on her last release from rehab, she was supposed to go into a sober living house, but she had just disappeared. The family didn't know if she was alive or dead.

She looked closer to dead than alive, and Katherine was horrified. She was a terrible sight – thin, gray, and shabby. She seemed somewhat altered, although it was only 10:30 in the morning. Kathy hugged her, and she felt like she was made of dust.

"How are my girls?" she asked.

"They're beautiful and happy. They have loving husbands and children," replied her sister.

"Good," said Caroline. Talking seemed to be an effort for her.

"Mother?"

"She's not too bad. She's improved a lot, but it's a long road."

"You look wonderful. You have a good husband, don't you?"

"He is an amazing gift," Kathy replied.

“I have to go,” said the poor ghostlike creature.

“It was good to see you.”

Thoughts were rushing through Katherine’s head and heart. Her heart told her to take Caroline home and try to help her. Her head knew there was no hope of that, and she just couldn’t expose her household to the hell she would bring them. Decades of experience left her with no doubt.

She reached in her purse and gave her a fifty-dollar bill and her business card. The card gave her phone numbers but purposely didn’t show her address. “Please call me if you need me,” she said, hugging her again.

Caroline said, “You tried to help me in the beginning, Kathy, but it was already too late.” And she turned and walked away.

Katherine went to her appointment and tried to push the incident back until later when she could talk to Eddie. By the time that happened, she was wracked by guilt and paced endlessly while they talked.

“I know that there’s nothing I can do, Eddie. Mother has tried everything to help her for over thirty years. We can’t bring her here. She’ll bring in street people when we’re not home, and they’ll rob us blind…if she doesn’t burn our house down.

“My God, listen to me…she’s out there, dying in the streets, and I won’t help her. What kind of a person am I?

“I should have tried harder. I should have taken her for coffee and tried to get her to go into rehab again. I should have…” Kathy was getting increasingly agitated, which wasn’t like her.

Eddie was very upset to see his wife this way. He knew that she had done the right thing. “You threw her a lifeline,

Kat. She has your phone numbers, and somehow I don't think this is the end of it. My darling, you are a pragmatist, as am I."

He took her in his arms and pulled her down on the couch beside him. She relaxed against him. "Do you think Sharon or Theresa would have taken her home with them?" he asked.

"Not Sharon, for sure, but Dennis would. Not Theresa or Gordie. They have little children."

"Dennis would have his house filled with every hard-luck case he ever met if Sharon would let him," said Eddie.

"You're right," Kathy said. "She has my numbers and I will try to do something other than give her money for drugs or alcohol if she calls."

The phone woke them up at six o'clock the next morning. It was someone from Police Services, reporting that a woman had been killed crossing King Street late the previous night. She had Katherine's card in her pocket.

Eddie drove Kathy to the morgue to identify her sister. She had been carrying no identification, only Kathy's card. She looked peaceful when the sheet was pulled back for Kathy to view.

An autopsy would be performed, and Caroline's remains would be cremated. Kathy would receive the autopsy results and her sister's ashes in due time.

When Kathy and Eddie got home, they sat in their kitchen and had coffee and brandy. Kathy said, "What would Gabriel have done?"

Eddie thought about that. "As Din pointed out at the memorial gathering, Gabriel was a wise man in a child's body. He had the most tender heart, Kat, but he also understood reality.

"Do you remember when that really nice cat of Barbara's got hit by a car?"

"Purrdy."

"He was terribly injured, but Barbara wouldn't accept it. She paid a great deal of money for operations to save him, but in the end, she did him no favors. His jaw had been broken, and he couldn't eat without assistance or groom himself.

"Barbara was so upset, and she wanted another operation, which really would have just been cruel, but Gabriel talked her into having the poor thing put to sleep.

"And when that happened, she couldn't handle being there, so Gabriel sat with him, holding his little paw until it was over."

Kathy put her head down and cried for a long time. She cried for Caroline, her nieces, her mother, brothers, and sister. She cried for Gabriel and the dear little cat Purrdy. Eventually, she looked up and said through her tears, "I love you, Eddie."

That night, a group gathered at the Gascoynes'. There were Kathy and Eddie, her brother David and Susan, Sharon and Dennis, and via Skype on two laptops, Nicholas and Emma, and Theresa and Gordie. Everyone was aware of what had happened, and the meeting was to decide what to do about Barbara.

Barbara had been doing so well. Her health was good and her spirits much better. She wasn't drinking other than a sherry in the late afternoon or a whiskey on special occasions. She enjoyed her companions, and her family was happy and relieved.

What was this news going to do to her?

There was a lot of discussion. Some felt that she needn't be told. It had been so long since there had been any word of Caroline. How could it be a good thing to bring everything back?

Others felt that keeping the secret wasn't the right thing to do. And others warned that Barbara would be furious if she ever found out that no one had told her.

Eddie said, "I have a proposal. Let's present this problem to the wisest man we know and ask him to help us."

That would be Finn. Everyone agreed.

In a while, Finn joined them on Katherine's laptop. He had been given the news on the phone and offered his condolences to everyone.

"It's hard to be sorrowful now that the suffering of that poor girl is over. She was only eleven years old when the nightmare began, and it seems that she never woke up. Her spirit is free at last, and may she enjoy eternal peace.

"If everyone agrees, I will talk to Barbara. We have been friends for twenty years and have a great understanding between us. I believe she should know that her child has passed. I believe that her new life and newfound self-respect will help her come to terms with the conclusion to the story.

"And it is the conclusion to that story, the anger and pain and guilt and remorse, the terrible damage to everyone Barbara loved. I know you all. I know that you are all past it and are able to accept and return the love that surrounds you.

"If I might so bold, I would suggest that Caroline's ashes be given to her daughters to make a decision about what to do. I believe talking that through together will give them an opportunity to cleanse their hearts of any bitterness that might remain."

There were tears and gratitude to Finn. "Oh, Finn, I wish I could hug you," said Theresa.

"I'll do it when we see him tomorrow," said Sharon.

"Bless you, Finn," said Nicholas in Edmonton who was holding Emma's hand.

She was bearing up remarkably well and said, “Thank you for bringing Finn into our lives, Theresa and Gordie.”

“Isn’t he wonderful?” Molly joined her husband on screen.

Embarrassed, Finn rolled his eyes. “This is my PR person,” he said, and he kissed her.

Finn did meet with Barbara. He drove to Maple Lane alone the next Sunday after lunch. She was surprised to see him without Molly, and they walked out on the property to look at the hydrangeas to see how their colors were changing as the summer progressed.

No one ever knew what they said to each other, not even Molly. When they returned to the house, Barbara was a little wobbly, but she held Finn’s arm and came in announcing that Finn would be her partner at bridge that afternoon instead of Janet if Janet didn’t mind.

She played well and took her usual glass of sherry. When it was time for the ladies’ dinner, Finn bid them farewell. Molly was expecting him. He had had an opportunity to speak quietly to Janet, who was a retired nurse, asking her to keep an eye on Barbara because she had suffered a loss in her family.

“It shouldn’t be mentioned unless she brought it up,” Finn said, “but I sincerely believe she will be okay.”

And she seemed to be.

Sharon and Theresa communicated a little more often than usual. They hadn’t talked about Caroline in years. The memories were very difficult, and neither wanted to revisit them.

Theresa asked, “Can you think of one good memory?” Neither could off-hand, but they agreed to try before they spoke again.

The following day, each had a small offering. That made them feel a little better. “And I have an idea about her ashes,” said Theresa.

“What do you think about burying them under the Gabriel tree?”

“Why do you suggest that?” asked Sharon.

She knew Theresa meant the maple tree on her front lawn. “Because I think it symbolizes tranquility as the maple tree was Gabriel’s favorite. I also think it symbolizes peace and reconciliation because Billy gave it to Gordie as a gift.”

When Dennis and Sharon came with Fawn to Antigonish to celebrate their ninth wedding anniversary in September, they buried all that was left of Caroline under her grandson’s tree. Gordie had had a small oval stone polished and engraved with just the word “Caroline” because that was really all they knew about her.

October 2015

Theresa was a happy woman. She was a grateful woman who usually managed to keep the bad times pushed back, far back. However, today was the fifth anniversary of Gabriel’s death, and memories were washing over her like waves.

She stood in her kitchen, her children off at school, preparing Gordie’s special lunch. She thought about the children: bright and beautiful Molly, so much like her grandmother; Michael-Gordon, Billy’s boy, a reality that made her sad, but she was glad he had a loving home; and her muppets, Joy and Sean, aged nine and eight, well-adjusted and full of fun, the only ones who hadn’t known sadness other than the death of their brother, the only ones who had spent their entire lives happy and secure with both their parents.

She thought about the overwhelming love with which they had all been conceived and the hurt and fear and despair which had brought Gabriel to be. Had he really been an angel sent to her to help her through the nightmare that followed? He lingered long enough to inspire everyone he met.

She brushed away a tear that was trickling down her cheek as she poured homemade soup into Gordie's thermos. She remembered Gabriel skipping down the street as they delivered lunch to Daddy and sniffled a little as she filled a Tupperware with fresh fruit salad.

"Who lives in that house, Mommy?"

"Why are blue jays blue?"

"What do you think that cat is thinking about?"

The clock stopped her reverie. It told her it was time to go.

As she walked down the front sidewalk, she looked at the Gabriel tree. Its autumn leaves had all blown away in Tuesday's windstorm. Another winter was almost here.

Theresa walked through the chilly morning. Suddenly, she saw clearly that she would gladly suffer again all the terrible things that had happened if only she could reach the place she was in now. Gordie appeared in her mind's eye. He was smiling at her, his arms spread wide. She quickened her pace.

February 2016

Eddie was coming to Hamilton for two whole weeks. Katherine was delighted. Two weeks to be together, sitting up late, talking and drinking brandy, lounging in bed until they were ready to get up, visiting their loved ones. Eddie, of course, would be doing some work, but it would be more relaxed than his usual hectic schedule.

They embraced like young lovers when he came through the door. "Do you want a drink, darling?" she asked.

"Not just yet," he said. "I want my pussycat."

"My genius," she laughed, and they walked up the stairs.

After a glorious welcome-home celebration, Kathy asked him if he wanted a drink now. "Most certainly, my beloved. Do we have any champagne?" he grinned.

"Unfortunately, there is none on ice, master," she replied. "All I can offer is mundane Scotch."

"Well, bring it on, wench," he ordered, with his classic Eddie-smile.

As she prepared the drinks at the small bar, she heard him gasp. She turned to see him clutching his chest, all color drained from his face. She ran to his side to find him sweating profusely.

Instinctively, she rushed to the bathroom for aspirin and returned to put one in his mouth. She dialed 911. The ambulance would be there in a few minutes.

She threw on her clothes and went into the hallway, calling for Alex and Liam who appeared immediately, hearing the urgency in her voice. She asked them to watch for the ambulance and show the paramedics up to the master bedroom.

When the paramedics arrived, they transported Eddie to a nearby hospital. Alex was going to drive Katherine, but Eddie managed to say, "My wife…" and gestured with his right hand. She rode in the front seat of the ambulance.

At the hospital, he was immediately taken to a small room filled with monitors and equipment. Kathy was taken to a reception area where she answered questions. She seemed to be watching herself. She could hear her own voice but was not aware of speaking.

After a long time, she was allowed to return to Eddie. He was hooked up to a monitor and oxygen tubes in his nose. In spite of that, he looked a good deal better than he had. A nurse explained that he had had blood taken, and it had gone to the lab.

"I'm sorry, darling," he whispered.

A very young-looking doctor asked if he could answer a few questions. Eddie nodded.

"What do you do for a living, Mr. Gascoyne?"

"Real estate."

"Tell me about your day," the boy doctor said. "What time did you get up?"

"Three-thirty."

"After how much sleep?"

"About three hours."

"What did you do at three-thirty?"

"Some work before I went to the airport."

"Did you have a good flight?"

"Got some work done."

"Did you drive from Toronto?"

"Too stressful. Took a limo."

The doctor smiled slightly. "So you were able to do some more work?"

"Yes."

"And then?"

"Got home and made love to my wife."

"When did the pain hit?"

"About fifteen minutes later."

Katherine hung her head. She'd almost killed her Eddie.

"That's quite a busy day, Mr. Gascoyne. And I see that you are sixty-three."

"Yes, unfortunately."

"Are most of your days like that?" the doctor asked.

"Pretty much. Maybe not up so early."

The doctor looked at Katherine. She nodded.

"Do you drink much, sir?"

"No. Got to stay sharp."

"Smoke?"

"No."

"You look fairly fit. You must eat well."

"I try."

"Mr. Gascoyne, I have to wait to see the blood results, but I don't think you've had a heart attack. I believe you've had an episode brought on by stress and anxiety. Are you worried about your business?"

"Consumed by trying to downsize," Eddie admitted. "I want to come home to my wife."

"Well, sir, I suggest you slow down considerably, or your wife will be spending time visiting you at a cemetery. That's not what you have in mind, is it?"

Eddie admitted it was not. "I promise to try. You have to help me, Kat."

"We'll talk about everything," she said. She felt like she might faint from relief.

The doctor left them alone, saying he would return with the blood work results. He wanted Eddie to stay the night so that he could continue to be monitored.

The doctor's suspicions were verified, and Eddie returned home the next morning. A new chapter was beginning for the Gascoynes.

Billy used his cell phone when he was working or away from home. He preferred to communicate by landline or e-mail. His sons made jokes about him.

He picked his phone up when he went into his office the next morning, and he read the text from Alex about Eddie:

ECG attk gen hsptl.

It was dated 9:57 the previous night.

Billy went ballistic. He loved Eddie as if he were his father. He phoned his sons and got the unfortunate Liam on the line. "What the hell is wrong with you two assholes, texting me that message about Eddie? You know I don't carry my phone with me every fucking minute like you do."

"Sorry, Dad. I guess we weren't thinking."

"Is he okay? What's going on?"

"Kathy brought him home this morning. He's okay. It was just a stress thing, not a heart attack. She's going to talk to you soon, I guess. She was pretty freaked out."

"How did he look? Can I come and see him?"

"He looked fine. Kathy looked bad. He's supposed to slow down. Lucky he's here for two weeks. But good luck to Kathy, trying to get him to relax."

"I'm coming this afternoon when Kathy will have had some time to rest, and I'm bringing your mother. You tell them. Will you be there?"

Wisely, Liam said, "Yeah. We're working on essays." They'd actually been planning on going to the university to hustle girls in the Student Union Pub.

He added, "You can probably come any time. Kathy doesn't look like she'll be resting any time soon."

"I'll see you in a few hours," Billy replied, somewhat mollified. "Maybe Mike would like to come too and see his grandparents."

It wasn't as hard as everyone thought to get Eddie to slow down. The experience had deeply frightened him, and the thought of his Kat at the cemetery was too much to bear.

He had been making great progress in Vancouver, and he decided to turn everything over to Larry. It was a complicated process, but ultimately he was permanently situated in Hamilton. He had his Hamilton and Toronto properties, but Katherine had insisted on working through lawyers and property managers.

Eddie had always had mental pictures about life in the poor house after everyone had swindled him, but his wife assured him that, even if his worst fears were realized, they were still extremely wealthy and the poor house wasn't really looming in their future.

She also convinced him to get moving with the Foundation, officially appoint the Board of Directors, begin soliciting donations, and start with some serious donations. Easter weekend saw the formal beginning of Gabriel's Miracles. Finn was Chairman of the Board.

Next, Katherine booked a week's luxury cruise on the Rhine River followed by a week in London. This, she announced, was their honeymoon. Eddie had been too busy for thirty-five years.

They described their upcoming trip over dinner with Sharon and Dennis, and Eddie said, "I just hope we don't have to pray at sunrise." Katharine burst out laughing.

"I haven't thought about that in years," she said.

The last time Kathy and Eddie had gotten away, other than visiting Antingonish or Gatineau, was at the beginning of their marriage.

Eddie had been working on a deal involving a luxury ski lodge outside Vancouver with an older gentleman who was the leader of a group of wealthy fundamentalist Christians. They were considering the lodge as a peaceful getaway where they could meditate and get closer to God.

Eddie thought they were all nuts, but the lodge was worth millions. He lined up a minimal staff and invited the small group to come for the weekend. He had to be there and begged Katherine to come too.

It was a subdued gathering, no alcohol, no television, nothing remotely resembling fun. Even the meals had to be simple fare. The folks walked the property, which apparently was truly inspiring, and spent a lot of time in Bible study.

They all went to bed very early because they had to get up before dawn for their sunrise prayers. Eddie and Kathy were invited to join them, although they had the suspicious smell of heathens about them. Eddie explained that they were Catholics and would attend Mass at the church in a local town. Papists were almost as bad as heathens.

After evening prayers, the lodge was in silent darkness by ten o'clock. There was nothing for Kathy and Eddie to do but have prolonged sex. Unfortunately, their suite was next to the pastor's, so they had to be really quiet. Wicked Eddie kept whispering filthy bilingual things into Kathy's ear to make her laugh.

The next morning, after the group had worshipped at sunrise, the Gascoynes said they were going to church and avoided breakfast.

Sadly, it was too early for Mass, so Eddie and Katherine had sex in the car in the woods. When they returned, the leader said they seemed to be glowing with God's spirit, and Eddie said, "Yes, my wife said several times that she could feel the Lord inside her."

In the end, the sale was made and at the full asking price. Praise be.

Dennis and Sharon were hysterical with laughter.

"That's it," said Kathy. "I'm waking you up at sunrise every day we're away. Be ready."

June 2016

Billy had to drive to a greenhouse near Hamilton to pick up some plants and shrubs. M-G came along to help.

It was always nice to travel in the truck with M-G. It was nice and quiet, not like when Alex and Liam rode with them, endlessly nattering away.

When Kim wanted to push Billy's buttons, she would say that maybe they should have been hairdressers.

After half an hour or so, Billy said to M-G, "You know you're my guy, eh?" M-G made an affirmative sound, but he felt really happy. Billy didn't say sentimental stuff very often.

"Well, I've been thinking that you'll be seventeen in a couple of weeks and starting Grade Twelve in September. Maybe it's a good idea to make some plans for after high school," Billy continued.

"But I want to work with you," M-G said with a tinge of alarm.

"That goes without saying, but I want you to have some official academic credentials behind your name. A diploma you can hang on the office wall along with mine.

"You've been working with me since you were a kid, and you have a lot of knowledge. You also have a talent for landscaping. I've seen you sketch out a plan on the back of a fast food napkin.

"Would you like to go to Ryerson and get a degree in Landscape Architecture?"

"In Toronto? By myself," M-G sounded horrified.

"Then how about going to Niagara College for a diploma like I did?"

“Could I still live at home?” the boy asked.

“It’s a fair trip, especially in the bad weather, but I’m sure we could make it work if that’s want you want,” said Billy. “I did it, and I wasn’t much older than you would be.”

“Another choice would be for you to apprentice as a mechanic. You’ve inherited your dad’s mechanical skills. I’m sure cousin Luke would take you on at Canadian Tire.”

“I love cars and all that, but I want to work with you,” M-G reiterated.

“Then let’s try to make it happen. I want you to take over the business when I retire or die,” said Billy.

“You can’t die,” said M-G.

“Okay. I won’t,” Billy laughed. “When we get home, want to look at the Niagara College website and see what’s going on?”

When Eddie and Katherine got back from their utterly fabulous vacation, the Foundation had done some good deeds.

They had already been aware of some worthy causes and had moved ahead with donations for wide-screen televisions for the pediatric dialysis unit at the Children’s Hospital and a new piano for Gabriel’s elementary school (resulting from Barbara’s presentation to the Dunnville Chamber of Commerce). Finn had engineered a rapid restoration of the home of a single mother in the north end whose family had been forced out by a kitchen fire.

One family member had seen a documentary about three former Presidents of the United States working for Habitat for Humanity following the devastation of Hurricane Katrina. “Let’s check them out,” it was suggested.

It was a great idea. Gabriel’s Miracles had a good deal more to offer than money. There were so many ways to move.

The Foundation made a considerable contribution, and a number of the principals applied for active participation.

In March 2017, help was needed in Mexico. Habitat for Humanity suggested that a group of six might help in a house-building venture in northern Mexico for a period of three weeks.

Billy definitely wanted to go; March was his off-season. Dennis and Sharon booked three weeks' vacation. Eddie wanted to go too, but Katherine said she wouldn't let him leave her side, so their son Eddie Jr., a marine biologist with the Province of British Columbia, took some vacation and represented the Gascoynes.

Gordie couldn't take time off. A new bay was being built at the service center, and everything was chaos. He was deeply disappointed, but he felt he couldn't take advantage of Seamus' good nature. Phil, Shannon's husband, stepped forward to be number five.

Although Finn was seventy-two, he insisted on going along. The administrators had had dealings with Finn and knew that he was strong and vigorous. They recognized that he was a natural leader and knew much about many things. He was the sixth member from the Foundation.

During the next couple of months, the team members were individually interviewed and attended orientation sessions and team meetings. Everyone was extremely excited. On Theresa's birthday and her and Gordie's twenty-first anniversary, Kathy and Eddie, with the assistance of Kim and Molly, held a Mexican fiesta to celebrate. Eddie and Gordie, M-G, Alex, and Liam were the ones figuratively crying at this party because they wanted to go too. The anticipation mounted daily.

It had only taken the project interviewer a few minutes with Finn to recognize what he had been sent. He asked him to be site leader for one of the two houses being built. Finn agreed and received lots of reading material, websites to investigate, and was put in touch with the other site leader who had taken part before.

Dennis would be making a short documentary most of the time, but he would also work alongside the "grunts" as Billy referred to himself and the rest of the team which would include other volunteers and locals. Sharon would help out in the small medical facility.

It was an exhilarating and life-altering experience. They were building a simple fifty-four-by-forty-six-yard dwelling to a tight deadline. It was hard work in weather not as bad as the summer months, but plenty hot nonetheless.

They worked from sun-up to sundown with a short siesta in the afternoon. After their evening meal, they relaxed briefly and then crashed. But their satisfaction and determination couldn't have been greater.

Finn was their overseer and almost immediately caught the attention of the villagers. Naturally, he had been studying Spanish so he could communicate on a basic level.

Tall and strong, wearing his hard hat, carrying his clipboard, Senor Finn fascinated the little children who followed him like lambs. He had to explain that it wasn't safe for them to be on the work site, so they watched him from a distance. When he would move away to a bench for a bottle of water, they would swarm around him, vying to sit on his knee or next to him.

Soon, in the evenings, the women would bring their older children, particularly their sons, to be near him. Finn was embarrassed by the attention and asked one of the administrators why this was happening and what he should do.

"Their respect for you is so great, Finn, that they want you to bless their children," he was told.

"But I'm not a priest," Finn said in confusion.

"Just speak to them like you would to your grandchildren."

And so he did. He told them to respect their parents who had made so many sacrifices for them. He told them to be kind and support each other. He told them to never stop learning. Education would lead to a better life. The things he said echoed what he had told his own children, with a little bit of Gabriel thrown in.

In three weeks, the house was deemed "magnifico," and it was time to go home. Dennis had a great deal of film to edit and many wonderful personal shots of the team members and his father and his flock. He couldn't wait to get home to work on the documentary.

After a joyous reunion at the Toronto Airport, the team and their loved ones returned to Finn and Molly's home. The senior Gallaghers' friends and neighbors had put together an enormous spread of food from their own kitchens.

There was turkey and ham, Irish stew, vegetable dishes, salads, and a seemingly endless array of desserts. It was enough food to feed the entire village in Mexico.

Everyone dug in. The food at the building site had been sufficient, but plain fare. On the last night, chicken had been added to the usual rice and beans and greens, hog parts, or fish if available. Billy ate so much that afterwards he lay down on the living room floor, declaring himself a whale.

The mood was exuberant, and during coffee and dessert, the Nova Scotia Gallaghers called via Skype. What a clatter as everyone tried to talk at once! "We are so proud of you," Theresa said. "We thought about you all the time."

"Hey, Billy, how happy do you suppose Gabriel is right now?" asked Gordie from the cheering group.

"It's not like the olden days," Alex observed privately to his brother.

"You got that right," agreed Liam. "Back then, everyone would be bawling their eyes out."

Later that night in bed, Finn and Molly clung to each other. They had never been apart since 1970, and it had been hard. They made love, not with the urgent passion they had known when they were young, but leisurely and comfortably, a promise of love forever.

"I yearned for you every night, my precious one," Finn said. "I was remembering the person I was when I met you, a man with no heart. You have made me what I am today. You are my *raison d'être*."

"And you are mine," Molly whispered.

Young Molly was preparing to write her final exams. The years at St. Francis Xavier had flown by, and Molly had excelled. She was on the Dean's Honors List every year.

She had changed her mind about four years majoring in Education with a minor in Music. Her musical education was already at the point where she could teach music in an elementary school, and she opted for a pass degree so that she could get there sooner.

She was well known in Antigonish, a regular visitor to the local schools, seniors' residences, and the library, sometimes playing with her father. She loved the interactions, and everyone loved her.

Someone in particular loved her: Steve Byrne, a doctoral student at the University. She had noticed him on campus; he was hard to miss with his bright red hair and neatly trimmed beard. When they were introduced, she found him to be quiet and thoughtful, extremely intelligent, with an Irish background like her own. She thought he was the nicest person she had ever met, and the admiration was mutual.

The budding romance didn't distract her from her studies. Well, only a tiny bit. Her ultimate goal was to walk across the stage and be graduated *summa cum laude* and see the pride and happiness on her daddy's face.

And so it happened. Gordie cried, and her family members who had traveled to Nova Scotia for this momentous day all shed a tear, even Alex and Liam.

Months in advance, Gordie had booked a room at a charming local inn for the reception because he didn't want Theresa to have to do any work. There was a group of forty, and what a celebration it was!

This was the first time most of the family had met Steve. He was a big success, and he recognized them as a warm and wonderful group. He knew in his heart that in time he would be one of them as he looked at Molly who was aglow with happiness.

Early the next morning, the family met for breakfast at Theresa and Gordie's. Long tables were set out on the patio and porch. Seamus and his wife and Brendan and his family were also invited.

It was a beautiful day, and everyone was in good spirits. Over coffee and just a wee drop of Irish whiskey for some, Seamus rose to speak. "Molly, my love, yesterday was your day. Today, I have something to say to all of you.

"It's sad to admit that I'm getting on in years, but the truth must be told. I decided a while back that it's time to enjoy what's left of my good health. First, my darlin' Maureen and I are going back to our homeland for three months this summer.

I want to walk the Ring of Kerry one more time while I still can."

(Applause)

"I have made legal arrangements regarding my business, and I am pleased with them. I will remain owner. My son Brendan who has worked with me since he was a little lad and knows the business as well as I do – well, almost – will take on the role as Business Manager."

(Major applause)

"My adopted son – I hope you don't mind, Finn and Molly – Gordie will be Service Manager. He is not only a master mechanic, but he has what fancy folks call 'charisma.' The customers just love him."

(Enthusiastic applause)

"Stand up, boys, and take your bows. I know that this arrangement will be a success since these two have been thick as thieves since they were young rascals."

Brendan and Gordie stood up and high-fived and hugged to cheers and shouted congratulations.

In conclusion, Seamus toasted, "Here's to the continued success of the O'Connor Service Center. And *Erin go Bragh*!"

Afterwards, everyone headed out, Steve and Brendan driving two vehicles to the Halifax Airport, Dennis and Sharon and Fawn and the Gascoynes heading back to Ontario by way of Quebec City. Molly and Finn were the last to leave, having decided to travel around Gaspe.

They were very happy and suggested that they might fly down in September to celebrate Molly's birthday. "Thank you so much, my children," Molly said to Theresa and Gordie. "It was a truly wonderful time." And she hugged them both.

"Goodbye to you too, my sweetie pies," she kissed Joy and Sean. "We'll talk to you all when we get home."

"Thank you, sweetheart," Finn said as he kissed Theresa goodbye. He embraced Gordie and said, "I'm very proud of you, my son."

"I love you, Daddy," Gordie replied in a voice that shook only the slightest bit.

"Please come back soon."

"Drive carefully," Theresa called to them as they pulled away.

The RCMP officers arrived at Gordie and Theresa's home later that afternoon. Their faces were grim, and their news was horrific. Finn and Molly were dead, just outside Antigonish, killed instantly by a drunk driver who had crossed the line. Gordie sat on the couch ashen-faced, unable to speak. Theresa held him in her arms as the tears rolled down her cheeks.

She could see them as they were just a few hours ago. They were holding hands, smiling at each other. For almost fifty years, they stayed together. And now it was over.

Epilogue

"You look positively angelic tonight, my love," he said. "You have stars tangled in your hair."

"Oh, Finn, the things you say," Molly laughed.

"Are you ready for the next part?" he asked.

"As long as I'm with you."

"Here, take my hand, and let's go," he said.

***

The next morning, the announcer on the Cobh local radio station said several listeners had phoned in the night before to report a shower of falling stars over Cork Harbor.

One caller described it as a rare event, incredibly beautiful. Another called it a gift of love from the heavens.